Cover Copy

He will sacrifice anything to protect her.

As the daughter of a prominent New Zealand judge, Samantha Knight finds herself being stalked by the very man who has been acquitted of murder in one of her father's cases. When she escapes to the Fijian Islands in the South Pacific for seclusion, her bodyguard makes chase after her when he learns her stalker is in pursuit.

Brigs Brigstone has never let any client down, or allowed the innocent he protects to be harmed, yet protecting Samantha will be a mission all unto itself. Letting his guard down around her isn't easy, yet he's known her his entire life and the spark which has always existed between them is about to burst into flame.

Can he locate her stalker, and all while keeping her out of the enemy's claws?

Content Note: Novella of 18,000 words, with a sexy bodyguard and a hot heat level.

Books by Joanne Wadsworth

The Matheson Brothers Series

Highlander's Desire, Book One
Highlander's Passion, Book Two
Highlander's Seduction, Book Three
Highlander's Kiss, Book Four
Highlander's Heart, Book Five
Highlander's Sword, Book Six
Highlander's Bride, Book Seven
Highlander's Caress, Book Eight
Highlander's Touch, Book Nine
Highlander's Shifter, Book Ten
Highlander's Claim, Book Eleven
Highlander's Courage, Book Twelve
Highlander's Mermaid, Book Thirteen

Highlander Heat Series

Highlander's Castle, Book One
Highlander's Magic, Book Two
Highlander's Charm, Book Three
Highlander's Guardian, Book Four
Highlander's Faerie, Book Five
Highlander's Champion, Book Six
Highlander's Captive (Short Story)

Billionaire Bodyguards Series

Billionaire Bodyguard Attraction, Book One
Billionaire Bodyguard Boss, Book Two
Billionaire Bodyguard Fling, Book Three

Books by Joanne Wadsworth

Regency Brides Series
The Duke's Bride, Book One
The Earl's Bride, Book Two
The Wartime Bride, Book Three
The Earl's Secret Bride, Book Four
The Prince's Bride, Book Five
Her Pirate Prince, Book Six

Princesses of Myth Series
Protector, Book One
Warrior, Book Two
Hunter (Short Story - Included in Warrior, Book Two)
Enchanter, Book Three
Healer, Book Four
Chaser, Book Five

Billionaire Bodyguard *Fling*

Billionaire Bodyguards, Book Three

Joanne Wadsworth

From the Author

I hope you enjoy this novella, a taste of this series. The other books in this series are full-length novels.

Billionaire Bodyguard Attraction, Book One
Billionaire Bodyguard Boss, Book Two

Chapter 1

The journey of a thousand miles, begins with a single step.

Samantha Knight sank her toes into Fiji's wet white sand, in that sweet spot where the ocean gently lapped ashore and pulled back. Tropical sunshine and cool breezes surrounded her. Silence and peace prevailed. Mmm, this was the place where she would take that first step in her journey of a thousand miles. No more looking back over her shoulder. No more fidgeting. No more worrying about the man stalking her. She'd successfully gotten a restraining order against Gair Forster and he no longer posed any danger. Yep, she could enjoy this vacation without her usually ever-present bodyguard, Brigs, hovering over her too.

"Bula, Miss Samantha." A boy with dimples and dark brown eyes grinned through the rustling palm fronds swaying high within the canopy of a coconut tree. "It's bright out today, miss."

"It sure is, Naviti." She'd met the child yesterday when he'd aided his grandmother in bringing her wares to the beachfront near her bungalow. She'd had fun selecting some trinkets for her mother and younger sisters. Naviti's grandmother had even delivered the gift she'd asked to have handcrafted by one of the local village carvers. Her father would love the wooden gavel with its unique Polynesian etchings along the solid handle. As a judge, her father adored his gavels, and the piece she'd gotten him was a beauty. Hand to her brow, she grinned at the mischievous boy. "What are you doing up there, watching the ocean?"

"No, I'm watching the man marching along the forest trail from the resort." Barefoot, his toes curling inward and fingers firm on the bowed trunk, the ten-year-old bounced down. In his scraggly blue shorts and an oversized bright red shirt, his black springy curls bobbing on his shoulders, he sprang from the tree and dropped onto the sand beside her. "He's big, real big, with a gun. He's frowning too, looks real worried."

"What?"

"He's coming. Look, riiiight"—the boy pointed down the deserted beach of white sand and crystal clear water toward the tree line swaying thick and green near the forest trail she'd not long arrived along herself—"there."

"Samantha!" An echoing shout from a man who stepped clear of the trail, his hands cupped around his mouth and his face half-hidden in shadow under his black cap. Ben Hammers. She'd never mistake him for another. He was a good friend and Brigs's closest confidant, a fellow bodyguard who owned his own bodyguard firm. Brigs often worked alongside Ben, the two of them having known each other since their army days, before they'd given the army up to pursue their bodyguard careers.

"Here!" She waved and he lifted a hand as he spied her then jogged toward her in his chunky boots and black jeans, his camouflage muscle-tee flapping against his defined torso and his holstered gun tucked under one arm.

Surprise and shock flowed through her. How had he known to find her here? She'd taken such care in making her travel plans and keeping her final destination under wraps. She hadn't told a soul which island out of these three-hundred Fijian islands she was ultimately headed to. "What are you doing here, Ben?"

"I'm here for you." He halted in front of her, so beefy and tall.

"I don't need a bodyguard. I'm on vacation and Brigs has always been my bodyguard when needed." Except she hadn't requested Brigs's bodyguard services for this trip either, not when she no longer needed them.

"Brigs is still your number one bodyguard and currently scoping out your bungalow and ensuring all remains secure there. I came to fetch you back for him. Your restraining order against Gair Forster remains in effect while you're on home soil, although he flew out of New Zealand along with his cousin for these islands the day after you did and now his whereabouts is no longer known. Brigs and your father are both worried, as are Danny and I. That's why we've come."

"Even if Gair followed me to the main island of Fiji itself, he shouldn't be able to track me from there to this location. I could have gone in three-hundred different directions." Yet somehow Ben and Brigs had managed to pinpoint the right island she'd chosen off the mainland, so somewhere along the line she'd made a fatal mistake, although hopefully not an irreparable one.

"I'm aware, which made things a little more difficult for us to locate you, but Danny mentioned how you'd spoken once of this island in particular, that you adored its remoteness and intended on vacationing here one day."

She'd told Danny, her best friend and Brig's brother, years ago, about her desire to vacation on this island. She hadn't expected Danny to remember that though.

"We started with that hunch," Ben continued, "and managed to call through to the reservation desk from the main island and confirm your booking with the resort staff right here." A seagull squawked as it flew overhead then glided down and landed on the sand beside them. "You should have given them a false name."

"I did give them a false name, although they also asked to see my passport when I checked in for confirmation of my true identity. I told them to use only my false name for all registration details, and they promised me they would. I'm even using a secure Visa card for all the transactions I make here." She'd dotted every *i* and crossed every *t*, or so she'd thought. The breeze rose and whipped her dark hair about her face and she shoved the strands back, frustration bubbling deep inside her.

"I'm sorry, but the staff here went against your wishes and loaded your true name into their database." He gripped her shoulder and scanned their surroundings as another seagull zoomed in and landed beside the first. "Which means since we found you, so could Gair now he's within this same group of islands as well."

Gair Forster had been infatuated with her ever since he'd been acquitted in the murder case her father had presided over six months ago, and now, with his disappearance from New Zealand to these islands, it certainly appeared he was stalking her again. She should have requested her restraining order be extended to include other countries, only she'd feared changing it at the last minute might alert him to her intention to travel outside of New Zealand, so she'd let it pass and flown out regardless. "I need to ask the staff to change my reservation then, to reinstate my false name and remove any links to my true identity. If I can do that fast enough, maybe Gair won't find me here like you did."

"Brigs has already seen to that name change and we hope in time so you can remain here, but if not, then we'll need to ship you out to another secure location, which is why we're here. We have to take every precaution since Gair isn't alone." Ben dug in one pocket, pulled out a snack bar, broke it in two and tossed one half to each of the seagulls. The birds pounced on their treats, snatched them up and squawked as they flew away with their prizes.

"Three single days," she muttered. "That's all I've had to reach this deserted island in the middle of the South Pacific and now I have two bodyguards."

"Three. Danny came along for the ride too."

"What?" Danny might be her best friend and a bodyguard, but he'd known how desperately she'd needed this time away for herself. He'd ratted on her instead of calling through from the main island to give her a heads-up on what had happened. More frustration thrummed through her. "Where. Is. He?"

"Right here, sprite." A wave from Danny as he swung out from behind the very coconut tree Naviti had climbed, the local boy having skipped off into the trees earlier when it had become clear she'd known Ben. Danny leaned lazily against the smooth, curved trunk, looking all innocent. The stinking traitor.

She planted her hands on her hips and sent him a deathly glare.

"Hey, don't go looking at me like that. I'm not the idiot stalking you, just the squealer." Danny lifted one brow with a reckless grin. "Sorry."

"You're totally not sorry. I had options and you took them away."

"Except there's one rule we bodyguards never go against—the client's safety always comes first, yours more than anyone else's since you're my bestie, so once we discovered your location from the main island, we hopped straight over here. It was the only choice." He strode across, ducked his head and kissed her cheek. "So, how's the holiday been going so far? Did I miss anything interesting?"

"Grrr." Her growl fairly whistled through the tight line of her pinched lips.

"We'll find Gair and his cousin." He gave her another reckless grin. "Don't you worry about a thing."

"Don't worry?" Two highly-strung words.

"Danny-boy." Ben chuckled as he eyed Danny. "I'd duck if I were you."

"Don't you move an inch, you traitor." She swung one fisted hand at Danny but missed since he dived to the side and spit up sand as he rolled clear. Gah, he'd always been so fast on his feet, the big brute. "Stay still. I need to hit someone, and that someone needs to be you."

Laughing, Danny launched back to his feet and dodged around her as she kept punching nothing but air. "Catch me if you can, sprite."

"I'm not a sprite." Well, she was compared to him. They'd been the same size when they were five and starting school, but only a year later at the age of six, Danny had gained more than an extra head of height on her and had never slowed down on his growth since. He even matched Brigs and Ben in height, no matter the other two men had another ten years on him.

"Stop riling her, Danny." Ben bounded in front of her and blocked Danny from her next punch. Holding her arms, Ben continued, "Brigs, Danny, and I have every right to be concerned about you. You're more than a client. You're a friend, a good friend."

"Do I really have to have three bodyguards though?" She mock-moved to the left then jumped to the right and swung around Ben. She nabbed Danny's sleeve, but that's all she got as he darted out of her way yet again.

"While away from home soil, yes." Ben back in front of her, his short blond hair glinting from underneath the sides of his cap. "Gair Forster didn't fly out alone from New Zealand on his private jet. As I mentioned, he's got his cousin with him and Hugh Forster is as bad as Gair and well known for his big fists and dominating ways. That's why there are three of us here."

"Then I'll get a restraining order against Gair and Hugh, one which takes worldwide effect, then I'll skip this island for another and resume my vacation in peace."

"It could take weeks to organize such a restraining order, which is weeks you don't have right now."

Drat it all. He was right.

"Ben makes a ton of sense, right?" Danny slipped in beside her, dropped an arm around her shoulders. "C'mon, let's get you back to Brigs. My brother demanded we find you pronto and return as quick as we could. We'll be in trouble if we don't get back soon."

"I still want to hit you." She gritted her teeth and pushed that urge aside as he steered her back along the deserted beach toward the forest trail leading to the resort. She huffed and stomped along, Ben keeping pace one step behind them. Through the lush forest abundant in ferns and leafy tropical plants, she strode while high above, birds twittered in their nests and the crashing of the surf breezed through from not far away. This island was small and almost perfectly round, a mile at most from one side to the other. "I've not seen any sign of Gair Forster among any of the new arrivals to this island. He's not here, and I can guarantee that."

Yep, she definitely would've noticed him or his cousin if either of them had turned up here. Gair was impossible to miss, the multi-millionaire so icky-slick and polished in his appearance. He'd come to court each day during his case—where she worked as a fulltime court aid—decked out in designer suits and riding in flashy sports cars. At his side, his stocky cousin, Hugh, had worn dark leathers and a multitude of tattoos etched into his arms and across his neck and chest.

Goodness, how had she managed to make such a fatal mistake on day one of her vacation? She should have double and triple checked her booking hadn't been changed and not just to have expected the staff to abide by her wishes. She slapped the sides of her denim cutoffs, the hem of her lacy white swing top swaying as she reached the paved resort pathway. Through the manicured gardens, she wove then passed the empty bungalow next to hers, the long fronds of the palm trees rustling in the fresh ocean breeze.

On the wraparound porch of her bungalow, Brigs perched in black pants on the round wooden rail, one foot idly swinging back and forth, his sunglasses hiding his eyes, although even so, it was clear to see he'd narrowed his gaze in on her behind the dark lenses.

She clomped up the front steps and halted in front of him, crossed her arms and tried to give him her sternest expression. "I didn't make the mistake on purpose. I gave them a false name."

"I know, and I've had your false name reinstated." He pushed off the rail and stood, his towering height dwarfing hers then slowly, ever-so-slowly, he removed his sunglasses and hooked them in the deep V of his tight black cotton t-shirt. His intense brown gaze swept over her, from her head to her toes and everywhere in between. "Have you had any problems since your arrival? Has anyone approached you for any unusual reason, tried to steer you away from others so you'd be alone? Gair flew into the main island of Nadi with Hugh, which means we can't discount Gair using his cousin in his endeavor to get to you."

"No. I've not experienced any problems at all." She tapped one foot. "Other than discovering I'm being stalked again."

"We'll deal with the stalker." He stuck one hand in his pocket, withdrew two key cards and tossed one to Ben then the other to Danny. "I've paid for the bungalows either side of this one, both thankfully empty. You two can take one each and keep an eye on this bungalow while I stay here with Samantha. There's a ferry arriving at the wharf within the hour with new resort patrons on board. We need to make sure Gair Forster isn't on it."

"Of course." Ben pocketed his card, just as Danny pocketed his. They both nodded at her then strode off with a breezy salute to Brigs.

Grrreat. Time for her isolation to begin. She stalked toward her front door, still incredibly peeved that her vacation now included three bodyguards. "If you're staying here with me," she snapped at Brigs. "Then there will be rules."

"I'd expect nothing less." Brigs slid in front of her and blocked her path, his dark gaze capturing and holding hers with a driven intensity she'd only ever seen blaze to life within his eyes. With his voice rough and raw, he uttered, "Sammy, I need to know if you're truly okay."

"I'm fine, just peeved is all and since the ferry only sails in once a day, then how did you manage to arrive here before it's even due in?" She jabbed his chest, his very wide and immoveable chest. "Please explain that."

"I have several contacts in these islands and I chartered a seaplane with a man I implicitly trust—Wiremu Haka. Remember his name for in case you ever need it, and if you do, give him my name and he'll be at your side in a heartbeat. He can fly you anywhere you need."

"Ever resourceful, aren't you?"

"I try to be." His voice dropped even lower, to a bone-melting level and she shivered, although not from fear. Brigs had never invoked fear in her, just a deep well of wanting that she wished she could do something about.

Taking a long breath to clear her fuzzy head of that wanting, she lifted onto her toes to gain some extra height against him and this time jabbed her finger even deeper into his chest. "If you're truly staying here with me, then you're in for a 'no-holds barred' Samantha. Can you handle that?"

"I can handle anything you want to throw at me, but for now, let's get you inside and out of view." He opened the door and swept her into the bure with its white-washed walls and high wooden-beamed ceilings. The polished floorboards, of the same rich mahogany timber as the ceilings, gleamed, as did the smooth surface of the round mahogany dining table tucked in one corner near the tidy kitchenette. A cane screen divided the kitchen and dining areas from the main living space and she stepped into the relaxing area where plush white-padded couches were pressed to each of the three walls.

Brigs quietly closed the front door behind him then scanned the rooms, taking note of each window and door, as well as the big-screen TV mounted on the wall, not that he hadn't already been inside and surveyed everything since his leather-beaten duffel sat propped against one couch.

He was such a big man, heavily muscled and at least six-foot-four with golden-bronze skin compliments of the touch of Samoan ancestry flowing through his mother's maternal line. Even his black hair, now a good two inches longer than usual and almost brushing his shoulders, flowed in dark waves with the odd springy curl amongst those waves.

"Stay right there," he commanded as he eased around her, his hands skimming her hips as he moved silently to the window and cast his gaze out over the lush gardens on the right where another bungalow peeked through the thick foliage close by. Over thirty identical bungalows lined this ocean front and Brigs raised a hand and waved as Danny mounted the steps of the one next door.

Slowly, her frustration eased further and in its place, Brigs's close presence continued to flood her senses, just as it always did. She cleared her throat and he lazily turned and eyed her from where he remained by the window. "This is a one-bedroom bure, Mr. Bodyguard, so where do you intend on sleeping while you're guarding me?"

Back at home, she'd only ever needed him during the day, never at her apartment at night since it employed an amazing security team with no access permitted after hours to non-residents. This resort was far different though. Guests wandered about everywhere, weaving through the gardens to make their way down to the beach. A family of four strolled along the paved pathway between her bungalow and Danny's, the young children skipping ahead and squealing as they reached the white sand where the waves lapped gently into shore.

"You've got a king-size bed, so I'll take the other side of it, or the corner chair in your bedroom. I'll leave that choice to you, but I need to be close, and this living room isn't close enough."

"Then I vote you take the floor by my bed."

He chuckled, his smile going wide, just like Danny's did.

"I mean it."

"I know you do." He ambled across to her, dipped his head to her ear. "I've missed you, my little fireball, and your hot temper. You also said there will be rules. State them now and we'll get them out of the way."

"Rule number one. You need to stop calling me your little fireball. Rule number two. I like my hot temper and it's not going anywhere. Rule number three. You didn't do anything wrong when I was sixteen and I want you to admit that if we're going to be sleeping in the same room as each other." She probably shouldn't have brought that last rule up, but having him this close was doing a real number on her.

"I kissed you in your parents' backyard, while you were still a minor. I shouldn't have."

"It was six years ago, and there's still a ton of tension flowing between us. I hate that tension. It makes me feel like I can't express my true feelings around you." She snagged his black shirtfront, her constant need for him flaring to full and vibrant life, just as it always did. Oh boy. As usual, within a minute of being back in his company, she wanted him all over again. Stupid annoying want. Yeah, she definitely needed to address this tension, once and for all. "I've never told you this, but I liked your kiss back then. I honestly did."

"I did more than kiss you that night, Sammy, and we both know it."

"Okay, so you copped a feel of one of my breasts too. Not a biggy." And she wouldn't mind if he attempted to cop another feel right now too. "We're adults, Brigs, and it's about time we talked about our past and set it all behind us."

"I was ten years your senior at the time and should have known better." A tic pulsed in his strong jaw. "It haunts me, that look you had in your eyes that night. The shock."

"It wasn't exactly shock, and I'm twenty-two now." Okay, it had definitely been shock, but that emotion had quickly disappeared and become desire, an emotion which she'd carried around with her ever since. Yep, and now she was finally going to tell him all about how deep that desire actually ran. No-holds barred Samantha. With a deep breath, she let him have it. "I want you to know exactly how I feel about you. Back then, I got so giddy after that kiss and ever since, I've wanted you to kiss me again."

"I'm your bodyguard, which means there will be no kissing going on between us." He brushed past her and strode into her bedroom.

Gah, how annoying. He always disappeared on her when she wanted to get deep and meaningful, but this was one conversation they had to hash out. She followed him into her bedroom and halted at the end of her massive bed with its white-quilted covers. He wandered about her room, searched her attached bathroom then eased in front of her bedroom window and scanned the outside perimeter, just as he'd done from the living room. The late afternoon sunshine streamed through, the vibrant rays highlighting his form in vivid gold. She grabbed a deep breath and planted her hands on her hips. "Brigs, do I scare you? Is that why you won't open up about this subject?"

"You could never scare me." He slowly faced her, rested his butt on the windowsill and allowed his smoking-hot gaze to roam her body.

"It makes me really hot when you look at me like that." She fanned her face. "Like really hot."

He blinked, frowned, then shut the look right off.

"Don't do that. You're pulling away again, and you and I have been ducking and diving around our feelings for each other for years. It needs to stop and maybe now is the perfect time for that to happen, particularly since we're stuck behind these walls until we're assured Gair hasn't found me."

"I don't have any feelings for you." He pushed off the sill and loomed over her. Slowly, he moved his hand in a rolling motion. "But by all means, please continue."

"Umm…" She cleared her throat. "For starters, this resort is filled with a lot of single men. Did you know that?"

"No. Are you trying to tell me that you've met someone?"

"No, and that's because I keep comparing every man I meet to you."

"You should date other men." A firm nod. "I have no issue with that."

"Well, I did have drinks last night at the resort pool with James Diggins. He was nice."

"I'll need to run a security check on him." He moved across to the open bedroom door then stopped just short of it before glancing over his shoulder at her. "Is he the only one you wish to date?"

"I didn't mention his name because I wanted to date him, but to prove a point." Her heart heaved, the sting of his constant rejection twisting painfully deep inside her.

"You should see others if you wish to."

"Damn it, Brigs. I want to see you, for you to kiss me again. How many times do I have to tell you that?"

He gave her his back and disappeared out the door, although not before she caught the tense tightening of his shoulders. Her words had definitely affected him.

"Brigs, wait." She chased after him, swung around in front and hands on his chest, halted him in place. "I really want you to kiss me."

"Danny wouldn't be pleased if I tried to hit on his best friend. My little brother and you have been tight ever since you were five, always have been and always will be." Gently, he cupped her cheeks in his hands, his gaze softening. "Gair is a threat, perhaps even a deadly one. I can't forget him in this equation."

"Don't go bringing Gair into this conversation when we're talking about you and me." She rubbed her cheeks deeper into his palms, then softly sighed as he eased one hand around her nape, his fingers sliding sensuously across her skin.

"I'm your bodyguard." He crowded her back against the wall. "I'm paid to guard your body."

"You could guard my body from my bed if you wanted to."

"No." He shook his head, yet his gaze dipped to her chest then slowly, ever so slowly, he hooked one finger under the thin top strap of her lacy cotton shirt and moved it aside. He slid the strap down her arm and exposed the upper swell of her breast.

She gulped, her mouth drying completely out. "Keep going," she whispered, hoping beyond hope he would.

"I shouldn't." Yet he pushed the other strap down too, until her top slithered to her waist and clung to her hips.

She held perfectly still. Never had he gone this far with her before and she was incredibly worried if she said even one wrong word, it might snap him out of this spell taking them both.

"You should be wearing a bra." He squeezed his eyes tightly shut. "You've beautiful breasts, Sammy."

"Kiss them."

"Stop encouraging me." He opened his eyes, looked deep into her eyes. "Tell me to get back on the job."

"Get back on the job." She scooped her breasts and lifted them higher and as she did, his gaze zoomed right back in on them. "And I mean this job, of kissing me. You can start with my breasts."

"I told you—" He shook his head and moaned as he lowered his head toward her offering. "I can't..." Then he flicked his tongue out, swept it along the upper curves of her breasts and moaned again, so gritty and hard.

Oh goodness. Sooo good. She leaned her head back against the wall, her back arched as she offered herself fully to him.

"Damn it, Samantha. I told myself I'd never touch you again, not like I did back then." He nudged her hands from her breasts and took them into his own hands then head dipped, he suctioned his mouth around one peak and suckled her.

"That feels incredible." He was kissing her, or actually kissing her breasts, and she wanted so much more. "If you stop right now, I might just kill you."

"Hold on." He lifted his head and cold air assailed her. "Someone's coming." He hauled her top up with a fast snap, grasped her shoulders and steered her back into her room.

"Wait, what? I didn't hear anyone."

"Trust me, there's definitely someone coming. Stay here." He enclosed her inside her bedroom, his footsteps moving away from her toward the front door of her bungalow. A light breeze whistled through from under the solid wood she'd pressed her ear to, then the gentle murmur of voices, Brigs's the clearest of the two, traveled to her. "Do you have anything to report?"

"Gair wasn't among the new arrivals." Ben. Definitely Ben, his deep voice easy to make out. "I've also gone through the resort guest list and he hasn't attempted to make a reservation here. Danny's doing a physical check of the island. Where's Samantha?"

"In the bedroom, taking a nap."

"Good. I'm going to join Danny and run the visual check of the island with him. There's a village a mile away on the other side of the island and sometimes the odd resort guest stays there, or so Naviti just told me. He's a local lad of about ten and was with Samantha when we first found her on the beach. I thought the kid had wandered off after my arrival, only he snuck into the trees then followed us back from the beach to her bungalow to make sure Samantha was okay. He's a good kid."

"Tell him thanks for watching over Samantha for me, and keep me updated on what you find out after you've searched the village."

"Will do."

The door clicked shut.

She turned the knob and ducked her head out.

Brigs remained at the front door, his back to it and his gaze on her. He lifted one finger and wagged it at her. "Stay right there."

"Not a chance." She sashayed across the room, past the potted fern near the dining table and snuck a peach from the fruit bowl on the kitchenette counter before reaching him. She bit into it. "Sooo," she drawled. "Do you want to join me for that nap?"

Chapter 2

"I shouldn't have kissed you just now." Brigs pushed a firm hand through his hair and eyed Samantha. She was toppling his barriers one by one, barriers he'd spent six years erecting between them. Six years. One provocative kiss, and in all this time, he'd never once stopped wanting her. "My work is dangerous, and I'm often away on location with clients."

"I'm aware of how seriously you take your job, and I love that you do." She swished closer, her long brown hair swaying so damn enticingly about her hips, and those denim cutoffs of hers showing off two beautiful lean legs. Cutoffs that were also far too short. Yeah, if she bent over in them, he'd be able to make out the lower curves of her ass.

Nope, no thinking about her very fine ass. He frowned, forced his mind back on the right track. "That means I have no time for a relationship, not with any woman, not even with you, Sammy."

"You could make time if you wanted to, but I'm not asking for a lifetime commitment. All I'm asking for is that you join me in my bedroom. Maybe if we slept together this once"—she raised one sassy brow, her voice all sultry and hot—"we might be able to release this simmering tension between us. We could enjoy a short fling as such. What do you say?"

"You deserve far more than a short fling." He flicked the front door lock and marched past her into her bedroom. She deserved a man who could offer her the world and all she desired, although perhaps she was right in that if they slept together this once, then maybe they'd be able to release this simmering tension between them. One night. Surely, he could grant them both that in order to satisfy their desires, and hell, he'd already walked into her room.

Samantha followed him, one hand raised as she motioned toward her incredibly tempting bed. "Does this mean you're saying yes and agreeing to a fling?"

"Right now, I've lost all ability to continue saying no to you, so yes, I'm agreeing to a fling." He stepped up to her. "We'll keep this fling straight forward, about the sex and nothing else. After tonight, we go back to being friends. Can you handle that?"

"Wow." Her eyes went wide. "Yes, I can, and I can't believe you just agreed to a fling. Do you have any protection on you?"

"No." Cupping her tiny waist, he held her in place, the sweet vanilla scent of her perfume floating all around him. For six years, he'd wanted her, to have her under his body as he thrust his cock into her, for her to shout his name when she came and now he intended on giving into that want. She was getting a "no-holds barred" Brigs today too. "Are you on birth control?"

"Yes, but doesn't every man keep a couple of condoms in his wallet?"

"Not me, not when I'm on a job."

"You shouldn't be so diligent." She gripped the collar of his shirt and yanked. She popped the two top buttons and sent his sunglasses hooked in the V, flying. "Sorry, but I really want you and I promise I'm clean."

"I'm clean too." He arched a challenging brow. "You honestly don't mind doing this without any barrier between us?"

"The birth control pill I'm taking is sufficient." She shot him back the same challenging arch to her brow. "I'm willing if you are."

"I'm willing." His heart hitched with how willing. "How many men have you slept with?"

She frowned then shook her head. "Is that a question you ask all the women you're about to tumble?"

"No, I never ask that question. It's just that Danny's got a big mouth and doesn't always keep your secrets. He recently told me you've never done the deed before." Learning of that had revved his engine up as nothing else could. He lowered his head and caught her mouth in a hard, urgent kiss. He wanted her, desperately, and when she opened her mouth under the pressure of his, his blood roared through his body. It zinged all about, flushed through his dick and made it pulse with a raw longing he'd never experienced so fast before. Not breaking their kiss, he scooped her up, laid her on her bed and kissed her a whole lot more.

"I haven't done the deed," she finally breathed between his kisses. "So, can you handle a virgin?" She yanked on his shirtfront again, popped another two buttons until it dangled open by the last one.

"I can." He flicked the last button clear and shucked his shirt.

"If you ask me, this moment has always been inevitable." Spreading her fingers over his chest, she gazed into his eyes. "I like that you're going to be my first."

"I promise I'll make this good for you."

"You better." She grinned. "You're also getting rather serious. A fling is never so serious."

"Sorry. I don't mean to." He rolled onto his back and rolled her with him until she lay over top of him. With her settled above him, her eyes twinkling gloriously bright, she palmed his cheeks before sliding her fingers over the raspy stubble on his jaw. Hell, he loved how she touched him.

"I told Danny about that kiss six years ago, and he's teased me about it often over the years." She traced her fingers down his neck, touched her lips to his lips and when he settled his hands on her bottom and stroked over her lush curves, she wriggled her hips, her smile growing wider. "I can feel your cock jabbing into my belly. Can I touch it?"

"You don't need to ask my permission to touch me, not when I have every intention of touching you exactly how I've always dreamed of. No-holds barred for both of us tonight. You all right with that?"

"Yes, and it's about time we both got honest with each other. I love that we finally have." Slowly, she caressed over the contours of his pecs and abs, then swished enticingly lower, right to the waistband of his pants. Wriggling up, she sat astride his hips and settled her hand over his erect shaft under the cotton and pressed lightly down.

His cock stiffened and lengthened even further. Not surprising considering her innocent touch. He cleared his throat. "I need you to free me, right now."

"This moment feels big." She played with the button-zip of his pants and he got harder still. "Does it feel big to you too?"

"What feels big right now is my dick." A fling was a fling, about the sex between the two of them and he truly needed to keep all talk away from anything romantic, or at least he hoped he could.

"Are you trying to insert some distance between us?" With her gaze devouring him, she lifted her hand from his erection and stroked over his chest. "'Cause if you are, that won't work with me. I might want a fling, but I want all of you while I have it." She smoothed along his shoulders, down his arms until she took both his hands in hers and lifted them to her mouth. She kissed his knuckles, turned his hands over then nipped the callused ridges along his palms. She was exploring him and he couldn't halt her now even if he tried.

"I'm shirtless and you should be too, Sammy. Take your top off so I can appreciate those beautiful breasts of yours again."

"Since you asked so nicely, sure." She smiled as if she'd gotten her way with him, the little sneak. Even now she only played with the hem of her lacy top, lifting it an inch then lowering it again. He waited, as patiently as he could, until she finally drew the white fabric over her head then ever so slowly, let it drop into a slithery pool on the covers.

Her breasts were incredible. Twin mounds that sat full and high, with rosy tips going hard and pebbling tight. He cupped both mounds, flicked his thumbs over the beaded tips and grinned as her nipples contracted and tightened even further. "I'm going to touch all of you tonight, which means there's no turning back in a few seconds. Tell me you want this."

"I want this. I want you." She leaned her head back, her brown locks spilling across his legs behind her in a sensuous fall.

Damn. She was such a gorgeous vixen and he was one lucky man being able to claim her this night. He lifted up and latched his mouth over one rosy bud and sucked the treasure deep inside. He moaned his approval and she curved herself more fully over top of him, offering herself up in every way. Gently, he stroked the undersides of her breasts. Such perfection and she tasted incredible, like an elixir he wanted to get drunk on. He let his tongue roam over every inch of her breasts.

"Brigs?" She moaned his name.

"Yeah?"

"I'm burning up."

"I've got you." He rolled her from on top back onto the mattress then rose over her, took her mouth greedily with his and swirled his tongue deep into her mouth.

She kissed him back just as deeply as he kissed her, pouring her heart into her kisses and offering him such complete and utter devotion. He could do no less than offer the same devotion in return. He trailed his fingers down her belly, over the soft indents either side of her navel then flicked the domes of her cutoffs free and pushed the denim past her hips and onto the floor.

Heat pulsed from her entrance below and he slid one finger under the thin red lace of her panties and speared through her soft brown curls. More. He needed even more. Delving deeper, he dipped one finger inside her hot channel and breathed deep at the sheer tightness of her. He eased a second finger inside and she grasped his hand and kept it in place, whispered raggedly, "Whatever you do, please don't stop. I want to be with you tonight."

"I want that as well." He pulled his fingers free of her delicious heat, not that he wanted to, then divested her completely of her panties. With her body naked before him, he flicked the button of his black pants and shoved the zipper down. He kicked the cotton off, his black boxers as well then gripped his shaft.

"Mmm, I definitely want what you've got on offer there." She licked her lips, pushed up with her elbows underneath her and eyed his shaft. "Can I suck on you?"

"Not tonight you can't." He'd never last more than a second if she wrapped her lips around him. "Take me in your hand if you want."

"Okay." Giddily said as she wrapped her fingers around his shaft, right over his fingers and as he eased his hand away from underneath her grip, she smiled and stroked his length.

She caressed him with such sweet pressure, rolled her thumb over his head and wiped the bead of pre-come from the tip. Over and over, she worked him, each pull growing stronger and longer. She built the buzz at the base of his balls to a whirlwind of heat and he gritted his teeth, the pleasure of her touch almost undoing him.

"That's enough." He jerked back, swooped down on her, his swift move making her squeal as he blazed a scorching trail of kisses down her neck and across her breasts.

"You're gonna make the perfect first lover." She slid her eyes shut and stretched.

His cue of her complete acceptance, and he took it. In a sweeping pattern, he licked across each nipple then dipped down her body to her navel. He nibbled on the soft skin of her middle and when she pushed her hands into his hair, her body relaxed completely under his and he went even lower.

He gripped her legs, pushed them wider and settled his body in between her inner thighs. His mind raged at him to take her, to claim every single inch of her, both with his mouth and his tongue. This is where he'd start that claiming. He parted her folds then with one long and sure lick, he lapped at her sweet entrance.

She bucked, her hips arching with each swipe of his tongue, her fingers digging deeper into his hair. "Oh boy, too much, too much." Her head fell back onto the pillow. "Slow down, Brigs."

"I've only just started, so there'll be no slowing down. Just hold on for the ride, my little fireball." Smiling devilishly—since he couldn't help it—he returned his attention to her womanhood and dived onto her clit. He sucked it deep into his mouth, lifted her bottom higher and fed his longing.

His physical need for her doubled, then tripled, and the moment she cried out his name and trembled underneath his tongue, her first orgasm taking her so swiftly, he reared up and gripped her hips. He teased his cock along her wet folds. "Open as wide as you can and don't tense up. I need you to stay relaxed."

"I can do that." She spread her legs farther apart as instructed. "I know there'll be a little pain the first time, but I'm ready for it."

"Hopefully the pain won't last for long, not since I intend on wringing another orgasm out of you yet." Covering her mouth with his, he kissed her with a wicked dance of his tongue over hers. Distract her mind, he would, and when she licked his tongue in return, he pushed against her thin barrier below and unable to hold back a moment longer, tore through her innocence in one fast thrust.

"Oh, wow," she gasped, her words muffled against his neck as she held on piercingly tight, her legs wrapped around the backs of his legs and her fingers digging into his biceps. "You're definitely a big man, but glad I am that you fit."

"I'll take this gently now, until you're ready for more." He pulled back, until he'd nearly come out of her, then ever so slowly sank back inside her. "Tell me if you feel too much pain."

"The pain is receding, and I feel as if you're not going fast enough." She clutched his butt and urged him to move faster. "I want more. Give me more."

With his hands on the mattress either side of her head, he eased up then pushed back in again. He rocked into her in a sensuous drive as he built his pace. Over and over, he thrust, until his balls pulsed with need and his shaft tightened something fierce.

"Sooo good. Go faster again." She moaned her pleasure and he increased his speed, his mind consumed by her, the only woman he'd ever desired. It had always been her he'd dreamed of each night, and had each one of these past six years. He pounded into her, harder and deeper, each of his strokes a claiming and one she met in return. "Brigs, please, I feel too much. I can't hold on any longer."

"Neither can I. Let go and I'll soar right along with you." Driving deeper, he reached down between then and caressed her clit and the second he did, she screamed his name, her inner muscles clenching down on him and dragging him into place. He bucked into her and her channel contracted wickedly around him with such intense spasm after spasm.

No more could he hold back.

His essence spurted from him and coated her deep inside.

Immense pleasure and happiness surged within him, her soft cries of delight such music to his ears.

Fully spent, he slumped on top of her and nuzzled her neck, his cock still buried deep within. Never had such bliss rolled through him. This was paradise, unlike any he'd ever experienced before, the kind of paradise a man could get addicted to, and the kind a man couldn't survive without.

Chapter 3

Samantha couldn't move with Brigs a heavy weight on top of her, not that she was complaining. That she'd never do, and wow, never in her wildest dreams had she thought her first time would be so amazing. What he could do with his hands and mouth was incredible, the best kind of incredible there ever was and he was grinning. She couldn't miss that wicked smile kicking up his lips. She stroked along his broad shoulders, his skin damp and their flesh still joined below, their bodies all sticky and warm. In his ear, she whispered, "I like having you on top of me."

"Am I too heavy?"

"The heaviness is perfect, so don't move." She stretched and smiled, all while still clinging to him. "Can we do that again?"

"What you need right now is a shower, not more sex. The hot water will help ease any soreness far quicker than anything else can."

"Well, I'm all for a shower, provided we shower together."

"You got it." He slowly pulled out of her, a grimace slashing his face as he freed himself.

"Is everything okay?"

"Yeah, I just didn't want to lose this connection with you so soon." He held out his hand once he'd straightened. "Coming?"

"Yes." She hadn't wanted to lose their connection either. She placed her hand in his and he tugged her to her feet then with one hand at her back, he ushered her into the attached coral-colored bathroom with its glass shower and sparkling white vanity.

He opened the shower door, flicked the lever on and stuck his hand under the spray and once the water had warmed, he motioned her inside.

"Have you ever showered with a woman before?" She stepped in and faced the heady stream of water. It splashed her front, while he eased in behind her and warmed her back.

"No, I actually haven't." He nabbed the bar of soap from the shelf and lathered it between his hands then smoothed the bubbles down her spine and circled her lower cheeks.

"Which means I'm your first in the shower." A grin as she turned around and looped her arms around his neck. "I like that."

"So do I." With his chest, he pushed her up against the glass and captured her mouth with his, the water jetting off his shoulders and spraying over her. He breathed heavily as he slowly pulled away. "I'm going to clean your front now. Say yes."

"Yes, and take your time. Please, take your time."

He worked more bubbles with the soap, his cock hardening as it rose from between his legs and waved high at her. Slowly, he soaped her breasts, gently circled each nipple with such incredible care then he hunkered down, going lower as he swept his hands down her belly, over her hips and along the sensitive skin of her inner thighs.

"That feels wonderful." A little blood washed away and on a long moan, she wriggled her back against the glass and flattened her hands against the shower wall behind her. "I definitely want to shower with you again."

"You're almost clean." He ran his fingers through the curls covering her sex, nabbed the shower nozzle, splashed water there then pressed a soft kiss against her mound before setting the nozzle back in place. Standing eye to eye with her, he cleared his throat. "I'm honored to be your first. You know that, right?"

"You're getting all serious on me again."

"I can't help it." A low growl then he kissed her again, his mouth moving over hers in a sweet dance, although all too soon, he broke their kiss. Without a word, he flicked the lever off and opened the shower door. From inside the white vanity, he plucked a fluffy pale blue towel and smothered her in it before guiding her into the bedroom.

Out the window, the skies had darkened and the stars had come out to play. She drew the cream curtains together and flicked the wall lamp on. "Time clearly flies when one is having fun."

"Are you hungry? I could order us a meal." He wandered—all gloriously nude and his bronze skin glistening wet—to the side table and picked up the black leather folder holding the resort's info, which included the room service menu. He thumbed through the pages, his rock-hard stomach rippling with defined muscle and the deep V of his sculpted abs making her mouth water.

"I'm starving, but honestly, not for food." She flicked her towel off and got as naked as he was.

"Samantha, wait." He dropped the folder and it thumped to the wooden floor, his gaze glued to her breasts as he raised a hand. "You need some time to heal."

"You promised me a fling and you need to deliver. Surely we can have some fun in other ways." She sashayed up to him, wrapped her fingers around his erect shaft and stroked him from root to tip and as she did, he chased her move with his hips. His cock wept from the tip, his length so ridged and firm.

"You learn fast, and yes, there are other ways." He latched his mouth onto her neck, sucked her skin into his mouth and left a big red mark behind when he released her.

"Stay with me tonight, and"—she shouldn't ask, but she couldn't help it—"tomorrow night too."

"Your offer is incredibly tempting." He slid his hand down her belly and cupped her between her thighs. He circled her clit, bent and captured her nipple with his mouth and scraped his teeth over the pebbled tip. He took her deep inside his mouth then sucked hard and her toes curled inward and dug into the plush sheepskin mat under her feet. "How close are you?" he muttered against her breast.

"Very close." This was a dream, to have his hands and mouth on her, and she'd take it for however long she could get it. "I love it when you suck on my nipples."

"I'm sure I love it more." He took the tightening tip of her nipple even deeper into his mouth before releasing it with a fierce growl. "Do you trust me?"

"With my life."

"Then let me make love to you so you no longer have to experience any pain. I want to make sure you heal without any issue." He eased down onto the edge of the bed, pulled her onto his lap, but not face to face as she'd expected, but rather with her back to his chest and the large floor-length mirror hanging on the far wall reflecting their images. With his gaze on hers in the mirror, he spread her legs wider and ran his finger through her heat.

Sweet need raced through her, her deep desire for him soaring fiercely to the surface.

"I like watching you come." Gold flecks blazed in his molten-brown eyes. "You're so beautiful, every single inch of you. I want to bring you to the brink of pleasure again, then send you toppling over. Are you ready?"

"Yes." She'd never give him any other answer.

With his hair disheveled and wild and sexy, he flexed his biceps as he pushed his finger deeper inside her. At her back, his cock throbbed with heat and she reached behind her, wrapped her fingers around his heavy length then lifted from his lap and positioned the head of his shaft at her entrance where his finger still played inside her.

In the mirror, he shook his head. "No penetration, although we can both find our release in other ways."

"I truly want to feel you inside me again. You are far too overprotective."

"Being overprotective comes with the job." He grasped her hips, lifted her clear of his lap and toppled her back onto the bed then he moved in over top of her and captured her mouth with his.

He kissed her and she smoothed her hands over the muscled breadth of his chest, the springy curls tickling her fingers and greedy for even more of him, she stroked over his wide shoulders, traced along the bulging contours of his biceps and forearms then swept her hands over his hips and along his groin. She cupped his balls in one hand as they dangled, the fine hairs covering them silky smooth and as she caressed them, his balls drew even tighter and higher, his cock growing longer and the hunger in his eyes blazing so vivid and bright. "Do you like this kind of touch?"

"I love it." He eased back until he knelt between her legs then he scooped her bottom, caressed her lower cheeks and lowered his head. He puffed hotly against her belly, nibbled down lower and whispered huskily, "I love touching you like this too, and putting my mouth on you."

"Me too." Her heart clenched with how much she loved it.

"I've gotta make you come again." He glided his fingers along the inside of her thighs, pushed her legs even farther apart and plunged one finger inside her. He stroked deep, until he hit a spot that made her cry out then pant madly for more.

Oh boy. She felt too much. Heat pummeled her and her blood raced through her body.

Eyes closed, she held on as he nuzzled along her inner thighs, his breath hot and his body even hotter as he rubbed her clit with his thumb. "Please, Brigs." She gripped his shoulders. "I need all of you, your cock inside me too."

"Don't hold back. Seek your pleasure from my touch." He licked her flesh with one hearty swipe, his tongue penetrating deep and such exquisite pleasure roared through her.

"I need—"

He sucked on her nub and her core pulsed.

She shattered as wave after wave of pure bliss took her and she lifted free of her body and flew toward the stars. A bright burst of colors zinged all about and as he lifted up and took her mouth in a hot kiss, she wrapped her hand around his length and allowed her instincts to take over. Stroking him, she increased her rhythm until he tightened his butt cheeks and pushed his hips into her hips.

"Stroke me faster, harder," he rumbled in her ear.

She did and he rubbed his thumb over her sensitive clit once more, each of his masterful caresses making her climb right back to the heights she'd not long soared from.

Pain, be damned. She needed him inside of her right now and since he was worried about causing her more pain, she'd take the option from him. She shoved against his chest, pushed him over onto his back then kissing him, impaled herself on his cock. Intense pleasure-pain assaulted her and clinging to him, she rode him hard, just as she desired. More. Faster, harder. She wanted to feel his essence spurt into her.

"Ah hell, I should have kept my eyes on you." He gripped her hips and kept her moving to the wild pace that had already taken ahold of her, then with a deep drive of his cock to just the right spot, her channel contracted something fierce and she pulsed around him.

He came when she did, shouting her name and shooting into her, his mouth on her neck as he sucked on her skin.

Such a raw and primitive joining.

Her body thrummed as she slowly came back down, then everything darkened as exhausted, she collapsed on top of him. Such sweet darkness. She sank into the oblivion of sleep awaiting her.

Chapter 4

Brigs stirred the next morning as a touch of sunlight slanted through the curtains where Samantha hadn't quite pulled them completely shut the night before. At his side, she lay, her chocolate-brown hair a tumbled mess and the white cotton bedsheet covering only one of her breasts, the other hidden by his big hand curled around it. She had such beautiful creamy skin, soft and smooth compared to his own tougher bronze skin.

Making love to her last night had been magical, and when she'd taken him into her body a second time by impaling herself on his cock, even more so. Thankfully he hadn't hurt her any further. She was such a vixen.

A knock rattled the front door, a series of three short raps followed by a final tap which always signified Ben's distinct knock. Danny always let out a cherry whistle with his knock to warn of his arrival, but no whistle reached him. Ben alone awaited him outside.

He swung his legs out of bed, scooped his boxers and stepped into them before zipping up his black pants. Barefoot, he closed the bedroom door without even a snick then checked through one of the windows overlooking the porch. Definitely Ben. He stood leaning against the railing in navy shorts and a dark muscle-tee, his sunglasses covering his eyes against the bright morning sunshine, his gaze alert on the beach and swaying palms.

He opened the door and joined Ben on the porch, pressed his hands firm to the railing as he leaned on it. "Morning. Have you got an update?"

"Sure have." Ben continued scanning the beach. "Danny and I passed around a photo of Gair Forster at the village and got confirmation he's never been seen on this island. This morning I returned to the wharf when a seaplane flew in."

"A seaplane?" That didn't sound good.

"Yeah, with Hugh Forster on board. No sign of Gair though, so maybe he sent Hugh out scouting." Ben cleared the growl from his throat. "Danny's watching him now. I came to warn you of his arrival, which means we need to leave, and preferably before Hugh discovers Samantha is here."

"Agreed." There wasn't a chance he'd allow his woman to remain here a moment longer, because where Hugh could be found, Gair was never far behind. Their enemy was closing in fast, something he'd never allow. "We'll take her to my island. It's not far from here, then one of us will return and deal with Hugh."

"I'll return." Ben slapped him on the shoulder. "It's been a while since I've been to your island."

"It's been six months for me." Which had been far too long. Work had kept him away from the island he considered his soul, an island he often brought clients out to. It was his safe-haven for them, the perfect destination for his current needs as well. "I'll charter a seaplane to take us there, through the firm I usually use—Wiremu Haka's."

"Good. I'll call Judge Knight and update him about what's just happened. I'll call the local authorities on the main island of Nadi too, ensure they know she's being tracked. We'll catch Gair Forster and make sure he doesn't get away with another crime again." Ben pushed off the railing. "I'll be back with Danny soon."

"Take care." He stepped back inside as Ben disappeared into the surrounding palms then he locked the front door and nabbed his duffel from where he'd left it on his arrival yesterday against the couch. In the living room, he stripped off, changed into tan cargo shorts and a white t-shirt then slipped his gun into the rise at the back of his shorts and tucked his shirt overtop. From the phone on the wall near the kitchenette counter, he placed the necessary call to Wiremu and for him to bring the necessary supplies he needed out to the island as well.

It was time to return to being Samantha's bodyguard and protector.

No more fling.

* * * *

Samantha stirred and stretched as a delicious new ache thrummed through her body.

"Mmm, Brigs?" She murmured his name as she rolled onto her side and languidly opened her eyes. Hmm, no Brigs, although he wouldn't be far away, not since he always took his job guarding her so seriously. She pushed up onto one elbow and searched the floor for his clothing. His boxers and pants were gone, although his shirt lay crumpled on the sheepskin mat. She eased out of bed, flapped his shirt out and slipped it on, the dark cotton dangling just past her bottom and the sides swishing open, the buttons scattered somewhere around her room. "Brigs?"

"I'm here." He opened the door and walked in wearing tan shorts riding low on his hips and his white shirt molded to his muscled chest. He crossed his wide arms and maintained his stance near the door. "Ben just arrived with bad news. Hugh, Gair's cousin and right-hand man, has just arrived via seaplane and Danny's keeping an eye on him. Hugh's alone, but I need you to get dressed and packed. We're leaving within the hour and flying directly to another island a short thirty-minute hop away. I've ordered breakfast and it should be here soon."

Her mouth dried out. "What? Are you certain it was Hugh on the seaplane?"

"Yes." He strode to her wardrobe, pulled her suitcase from the top shelf and set it on the bed. He unzipped the top flap, hauled clothes from her dresser and packed them inside.

Numb, she shuffled across to him, laid a hand on his arm. "Wait."

"There's no time for waiting. You need to get dressed." He pulled a pair of panties from the next pile he placed in her case, went down on one knee at her feet and held them out for her. She stepped into the white satin and he skimmed her panties up her legs then held out the matching bra. "Shirt off."

She removed his shirt and dropped it on top of her packed clothes while he whipped in behind her and hooked her bra into place. He selected clothing from her wardrobe, a short white skirt embroidered with hibiscus flowers along the hem and secured it at her waist with the ties then he buttoned the matching cotton top and placed a pair of leather flats on the floor. "Feet in."

"I can't believe Hugh's here. My true name has been removed from my reservation." She slipped her feet into her flats.

"He either discovered you were here before I asked for the change to be made, or he's working his way through the islands one by one and managed to strike it lucky."

"What about your trail? Did you leave one from the mainland to this island?"

"No, I never leave a trail." He popped a kiss on her forehead. "You know me better than that, Sammy."

"Yes, I do. I'm sorry. I shouldn't have even asked that question." She tried to force the numbness aside. She was safe. Brigs, Ben, and Danny were here and they'd never let anything happen to her. She had three big and bossy bodyguards which beat one stalker and his evil sidekick.

Determination fired inside her and she gathered her resolve and walked into the bathroom. She pulled her brush through her hair and tidied it as best as she could before cleaning her teeth and gargling mouthwash. Once she'd packed her toiletries away in her toiletry bag, she added it to her suitcase and Brigs zipped it up and with the case's square handle in hand, carried her belongings out into the main room.

Brigs set her case beside his duffel near the door then opened it as footsteps clacked across the porch. A young female staff member dressed in the resort's yellow and red floral skirt and shirt, handed him a tray, dipped her head and wished them a good morning.

Brigs set the tray on the dining table, shut the door and pulled out a chair for her. "Take a seat."

Her appetite had disappeared the second he'd said Hugh's name, but she sat anyway and stared at the tray with the metal dome over top of it. "I'm not hungry."

"You missed dinner and I won't allow you to miss breakfast too." He stood over her from behind, his hands firm on her shoulders. "Everything will be all right."

"Yes, it will, because you're here." He'd never let anything happen to her. That she knew to the depths of her heart. She lifted the dome and the savory aroma of bacon and eggs swirled through the air. Fresh bread, toasted and buttered, sat to the side. She patted the seat next to her. "Please, sit."

"Give me a second." He strode into the small kitchenette to the side of the dining area and returned with two bottles of water from the bar fridge and cutlery and plates from the cupboard. He set everything down before taking the seat next to hers.

She forked some of the bacon and eggs onto one bread slice and folded it in two. Taking a big bite, she eyed Brigs as he did the same. "What's our next course of action once we reach this island you spoke of?"

"Ben will return and deal with Hugh. We need undeniable proof that Gair and Hugh are attempting to find you, even more than what we currently have. Once we've got that, then we'll inform the authorities and work from there. I won't allow either of those two men anywhere near you."

"I know you won't." She had complete faith in him, always had and always would. She sighed as she rested back into her chair and forced another bite down.

A cherry whistle drifted to her from outside. Danny's whistle. She'd never mistake it, and neither did Brigs since he didn't move but simply called out, "Come in, Danny."

With his army duffel over one shoulder, Danny breezed through the door wearing casual cobalt shorts with a wide leather belt and a V-necked tee. Turning the cap on his head backwards, he dropped into the wooden-back chair on the other side of her and scraped his seat right up against hers. Danny pinched her bacon and egg sandwich, took a big bite and passed it back to her. "You look a little numb, sprite."

"I'm gonna miss this place, that's all." She leaned her head against his shoulder and softly sighed as he draped one arm around her back.

"Everything will be all right. We'll slip away from this joint, go live in the lap of luxury on Brigs's island in his swanky digs, and party-it-up."

"What do you mean by Brigs's island?" She sat straighter, frowned at Danny. "Your brother doesn't own an island." She would have heard about that if he did.

"It's his little secret, but he does own a tropical island. Six hectares altogether, with one massive mansion and a tennis court and pool. He stays there from time to time. So have I." The firm expression on his face said he wasn't lying either.

"I didn't know." She faced Brigs. Sure, he had a lot of money and always had, even owned the penthouse suite in an exclusive building right on Auckland's waterfront, although owning an entire island was on a whole other level to owning a penthouse suite. She snorted under her breath at him. "And to think you made me pay for dinner the last time we ate out together. You scrooge."

"We ate at a burger joint."

"I still paid."

"I didn't have my wallet on me, and I'll shout you a burger the next time we eat out." He munched on his breakfast and snarled at Danny. "Stop getting me into trouble."

"You better believe you'll pay." She flicked Brigs in the arm. "And I'll want fries with that burger too, and a large chocolate shake. I won't be sharing my shake either." She tore off another bite and chewed. "So, how often do you holiday on your island?"

"He's often there." Danny winked at her. "He never talks about the place because firstly, it means a heck of a lot to him, and secondly, he uses it primarily as a safe-haven for clients."

"Oh, now I see why you've both never mentioned it." Neither Danny or Brigs would ever tell her the location of any safe-house, no matter if Brigs personally owned it. She popped a kiss on Danny's cheek. "I'm really glad you're here right now, but you should know I kissed your brother last night and I really liked it."

"You did?" He swiveled around and arched a brow at Brigs. "This true?"

"Yes." Brigs munched on his breakfast then took a swig of water.

"Well, I can only say it's about time. You two have been ducking and diving around each other for years." A grin from Danny.

"After we kissed, we also slept together." She'd never be able to withhold that kind of information from her best friend.

"Whoa." He blew out a long breath. "Kissing then jumping straight into sex is huge. Was he gentle with you? It's not like you've done it with anyone else before."

"He was gentle and fantastic." She couldn't keep that news in or the exuberance from her voice, no matter how private the subject was. She and Danny shared everything, well, other than for the fact that his brother was rolling around in so much dough he'd actually bought an island, but she could forgive him for not mentioning that.

"It was also a one-time thing, Danny, nothing more than that." Brigs stood and crossed to the open door as more footsteps drifted toward them.

"Somehow," Danny whispered as he leaned into her ear, "I doubt it'll be a one-timer. He's wanted you for years, six years to be precise."

Ben walked in and cast his gaze over each of them. "Our ride is coming in now, guys."

The soft hum of an engine rumbled and a seaplane swooped in and glided across the waves. It skimmed the surf and roared right up onto the shore before the pilot cut the engine. She rose from her chair and stepped in beside Brigs. "Door to door service. That's kinda cool. How'd you arrange that?"

"Wiremu is good. I gave him your bungalow's location and he knew exactly which stretch of the beach to fly to." Brigs nabbed his duffel, slung it over his shoulder and handed her case to Ben. Gripping her elbow, he guided her out the door as Danny breezed in on her other side and slapped his cap over her head.

"Keep your head down, Samantha." An order from Ben at her back.

At the seaplane, she stepped onto one floating side and Brigs settled his hands on her waist and boosted her inside. Once in her seat, Wiremu smiled at her from the pilot's seat and welcomed her on board with his charming grin and big brown eyes. She thanked him and then gripped the edge of the window as the plane glided back over the waves and lifted off.

The long length of the white-sand beach and the resort with its frond-roofed bungalows surrounded by tropical trees and bushes, became smaller and smaller the higher they soared. Her time here was done, but not her time with Brigs, a fact she'd hold close to her heart.

Yes, he might have insisted that what had happened between them was a one-time thing, but for her, it felt far bigger than that. He'd awakened her to a whole new world of loving, and she desperately wanted more time with him, time she intended on claiming, whether her bodyguard wanted to offer that time or not.

Chapter 5

In summery white shorts and a red tank top, Samantha adjusted her shades as she sat on the grass beside Danny, in front of the sprawling three-story mansion on Brigs's island. The wide array of the mirrored glass windows reflected both the ocean's waves and the vivid pinks and purples of the fragrant hibiscus bushes all abloom around them.

Five days ago, Ben had returned to the resort after they'd landed here, but unfortunately Hugh had flown out not long after they had and so far, they'd been without any further sightings of either him or Gair. So frustrating, and so was her bodyguard who'd remained detached from her ever since their arrival.

She pulled her knees to her chest and contemplated her next move regarding him. Even now, he continued to pace the white sand beach twenty feet away, not daring to come any closer.

"I've never seen Brigs this agitated before." Sprawled at her side, Danny knocked her raised knees with the back of his hand.

"That's because the authorities on the mainland have no idea where Gair and Hugh are any more than we do." She'd kept an eye on Brigs as he'd remained in constant contact with the police via the satellite phone he kept here. He'd been furious with the lack of their ability in finding their enemy.

"Well, the Forsters can't hide out forever within these islands." Danny shoved a hand through his hair, his dark locks a tumbled mess from his earlier swim.

"We're successfully hiding out, so I don't see why they can't."

"Yeah, but we have a place which is fully stocked with food and no need for us to leave." Sweat beaded on his brow, the late afternoon heat intense.

"Gair is a multi-millionaire," she counter-argued. "He could hide out for as long as he wanted, wherever he wanted. He's not used to being told what he can and can't do either, and I sincerely doubt he's ever heard the word *no* from anyone other than me. When he wants something, he digs in and goes for it." Which she'd witnessed time and time again during his court case. He'd approached her at least twenty times during those long weeks while she'd been working. Each time they'd spoken, he'd asked her out and each time she'd turned him down. She honestly hadn't been able to believe his nerve. She was a court aid and her father presided over his case. Never would she have been so unethical in agreeing to a date with him, yet he'd continued to act the innocent the entire time. How he'd gotten the jury to side with him, she still couldn't fathom. His former lover had died a gruesome death, and so many signs had pointed to Gair being the assailant, only none of the evidence put forth had ever been quite strong enough to provide absolute proof of his part in her demise. He'd been acquitted by the jury on that basis.

"You're the only one who has ever said no to Gair, that I'm aware of." Solemn words from Danny as hefty waves crashed against the reef a hundred feet offshore beyond the crystal-clear blue waters of the lagoon. "That's the allure you pose for a man who can have whatever he desires. With you saying no to him all the time, it only made his chase of you far more tempting."

"He's not the man I want to be tempting right now though." She leaned in closer to his ear. "I need to find a way to break down your brother's barriers. Have you got any good ideas? Because I'm in desperate need of some."

"I've got a few, but are you sure you want to hear them?" A teasing glimmer in his eyes.

"Only if they don't include anything illegal."

"First option." That glimmer brightened. "You could strip off and run along this beach naked. He'd be all over you then."

"I've actually considered that, but I don't want to give you an eyeful." She swatted his arm. "I wondered if I should cook him a special meal, something for just the two of us, but you and Ben would have to scatter so we could be alone after I served it. He's been so careful since we've arrived not to remain alone with me, like I'm some big scary thing that's going to bite him or something."

"You are big and scary to him, particularly since he's got such strong feelings for you. He always has and if he decides to choose you, then it'll force him to reassess the course he's always chosen for his life, his job as a bodyguard and all."

"If we got together, I'd never ask him to give up his job." That's the last thing she'd ever do. "He finds such pleasure in guarding and caring for others. That's part of who he is, and I've no intention of changing that."

"Maybe that's what you should tell him then."

She thumbed her chin, Danny's idea a stellar one, and if that didn't work, then she'd bite the bullet and run down the beach naked. She wanted her bodyguard, and she wanted him now.

"Hey, you two." Ben trotted down the front steps in black shorts and a cotton-ribbed red tee and joined her and Danny, his ever-present binoculars looped around his neck and his sunglasses slotted on the top of his head. "I'm gonna do another round of the island. Once the surveillance cameras Brigs ordered have arrived, we'll be able to set them up and maintain twenty-four-hour surveillance that way instead."

"How come Brigs doesn't already have that kind of surveillance gear here?" Hand to her brow, she raised her gaze to Ben's, the summer sunshine beating down and casting his shadow in a rippling wave over the dried grass. Only the odd patch of green poked out here and there.

"In the past, we secreted our clients here, so no need for any additional surveillance cameras. Things are different though with you. We need that gear here since your stalker has already followed you." Ben squeezed her shoulder then strode past her and joined Brigs down by the water where the waves washed into shore. Ben spoke to him, their words too quiet to hear, then he jogged down the beach and disappeared into the swaying coconut trees.

Brigs prowled up the beach toward them, propped one foot on the washed-up log in front of her then pressed the palm of his hand to his upper thigh, his sunglasses hiding his eyes as he tipped his head toward Danny. "I need to talk to Samantha, alone. That okay with you?"

"What? You do?" She shoved Danny in the arm. "Go, scatter, and don't come back for a very long time."

"Yep, that's okay with me." Danny chuckled as he stood. "I guess the little nudie-show doesn't have a chance now."

"Get moving." She nabbed his ankle and tried to heave, only he slipped right out of her grasp and bounded inside with a hearty laugh.

"Talk to me." Three stern words from Brigs as he lifted his sunglasses and slid them on the top of his head, his brown eyes piercing in intensity. "I know you spoke to your father this morning. What did Judge Knight have to say?"

Well, that wasn't exactly what she wanted to talk to him about, but she could start there. "Ah, that he's rushing through the paperwork on an international restraining order against Gair, and that he'll let me know the second it's done. He can't do much about issuing one against Hugh though, not until Hugh shows himself as being a threat."

"I see." He tapped his leg, his long fingers drumming away, fingers she hadn't been able to cease dreaming about each night when she'd lain alone in her bed. Geez, five long days. She was starved for his touch.

"Come and sit. I wanted to chat to you about something important." She patted the space beside her. "Please."

"That's all I needed to speak to you about, nothing more." He stepped away, slotted his sunglasses back on his nose and returned his gaze to the ocean.

She let out a loud harrumph, pushed to her feet and slapped her backside of the dry grass clinging to her. "You're a flippin' fantastic conversationalist at times, Brigs Brigstone." Although she wasn't ready to give up on him yet. "And by the way, if we got together, I'd never ask you to give up your job. That's part of who you are and I've no intention of ever changing that." She waited for him to answer her, except he didn't move, his gaze still roaming the water line. "Maybe I should get a restraining order out against you next, to make sure you can never step within one-hundred feet of me ever again. Would you like that, Mr. Bodyguard?"

She waited, hoping he'd take that bait and start talking to her again.

Nothing. Not a flicker of movement or the opening of his lips.

"I would do it, you know." She totally wouldn't.

He remained ramrod straight.

Argh. She gritted her teeth and stomped up the front steps. Better she walk away from him now to calm down for a second before she tackled him again. A swim to cool down would soothe her, which meant changing into her swimsuit. She took the curved staircase at the edge of the wide foyer up to the second floor. Plush white carpet graced the floors and stunning underwater ocean prints hung on the sandy-colored walls. In her bedroom with its four-poster bed and sheer white canopy flowing down each side which kept the insects away at night, she donned her pink bikini. She wasn't yet ready for a nudie-show, but she was getting close. She slapped on plenty of sunscreen and marched back downstairs.

Outside, she swished past Brigs, a coiled tension simmering deep in her belly. She opened the lid of the wooden outdoor chest holding an array of flippers and masks and selected the set she'd used each time she'd gone snorkeling with Danny.

"Samantha?" Brigs caught her hand, his voice so soft as he turned her around to face him.

Her heart somersaulted at his touch, that he'd finally made some form of physical contact. "Yes?"

"If you ever got a restraining order out against me, I'd break it in two seconds flat." He dipped his head and kissed her, with such a shockingly hard meshing of their mouths, then breathing hard, he pulled away just as quickly. "Ignore that kiss."

"I don't want to ignore it." She breathed just as hard as he did. "I wish you were the one stalking me."

"I need to keep you safe and I can't do that when I lose all control around you."

"You are keeping me safe." And boy, did she like it when he lost all control. "I can honestly accept your job, have no issue with you being away as needed. As long as you always come back to me, that's all that matters."

"I've never seen myself settling down with any woman, other than you, and that was far too much information. I shouldn't have said that." He pointed to the water. "If you're heading out for a swim and snorkel then go, but stay within the boundary of the coral reef of the lagoon."

She stood there and eyed him. She didn't want to halt this conversation, not when she was finally getting somewhere, only it was clear he still wasn't yet ready to fully open up to her. She'd have to keep on waiting, even if it killed her to do so.

Thrumming with even more frustration, she walked down to the water's edge, stuck her flippers on and walked backward into the waves. Once she reached waist-depth, she donned the mask and snorkel then turned around and dove.

The lagoon's sparkling blue water closed in over her head and she kicked along the sandy seafloor and tried to shake off her currently unhelpful emotions. Brilliantly colored tropical fish darted all about and even a stingray burst from the sand and glided away with a fast swish.

Needing a breath, she kicked to the surface and bumped into one shirtless Brigs, water sluicing down his chest as he treaded water. He nabbed her around the waist and she wrapped her arms around his neck, her heartbeat thundering in her ears. "Did you need to talk to me some more?" Oh damn, she hoped so.

"Yes, I'm tired of always wanting you."

"I'm tired of always wanting you too."

"It's been absolute hell keeping my hands off you these past five days."

"I hate the wall between our bedrooms."

"I'm gonna knock it down."

"You are?"

"Or I could leave it there if you invited me into your room instead." Such need flickered in his gaze.

"Okay, you're invited." She leaned in, licked his lower lip. "I want another fling, in case I didn't make that obvious, but a really long fling."

"I love you, Sammy. I always have and always will."

"Now we're finally getting somewhere." She shoved her hand down between them, pushed the waistband of his shorts out of the way and gripped his straining cock. "And now would be a really good time to show me some of that love."

"Honestly, I've loved you ever since I first kissed you, six long years ago." He kicked them a little closer to the shore and when his feet touched the seafloor, the water lapping at his chest, he set her down and under the water, swept the crotch of her bikini pants aside. "Put me inside you, and hurry it up."

"Yes, sir." She guided his length inside her channel.

"Ah, hell." A rough groan and he pushed deeply into her, then he lifted her up and dropped her back down on top of him. "You're impossible to stay away from."

"So are you." She lifted her mouth to his, stroked her tongue across the seam of his lips until he opened his mouth and kissed her just as ravenously as she kissed him. She moved over him, taking him even deeper inside her and as they kissed, a needy pressure built in her core. "I'm so close already."

"So am I, my little fireball." Under the rippling surface of the water, he flicked her nub and she cried out his name, her inner channel contracting so fiercely around him. He came fast too, right along with her and pumped his heat deep inside her.

Perfection. Such sheer perfection.

Never had her soul been so at peace.

Chapter 6

Later that night in Brigs's massive bed after a marathon five hours of hot sex, Samantha smiled as the stunning golden hue of the moon shimmered through his second-floor window and played across the contoured ridges of his abs. She leaned over him where he laid on his back, licked one flat male nipple and fairly purred her delight, his eyes closed and a sexy-as-hell grin on his face.

"Are you still hungry?" He opened one eye. "I thought I'd made a dent in your insatiable appetite for now."

"It'll take a while before you make any dent in it at all." She licked his other nipple then nipped it.

"I'm still extremely hungry myself." He stretched and squeezed her bare backside. "Wriggle up and sit on my face. I want some Samantha Knight served up, and I need it right now."

"That's actually possible?" She would have gasped at his outrageous words, only they'd made her flush with heat instead, and in all the right places. "So, you're saying I can actually sit on your face, right?"

"Absolutely." A chuckle. "And I'll show you how if you get moving. Crawl up and kneel right over my mouth."

Her belly rumbled and she giggled.

He arched a brow. "That sounds like you really are hungry, and for food this time."

"I am, so before I crawl anywhere, I'll grab us both some snacks and bring them up. After we've eaten, I promise I'll sit wherever you tell me to sit."

"Deal." He caught her hand, lifted it to his lips and kissed each of her fingertips. "I love you, Sammy, so much it actually hurts."

"I love you too, and that's what you get for denying us both of an actual relationship until now, but I promise to help ease that hurt if you ask nicely." Which meant she definitely needed some sustenance before she went another round or two or ten in his bed with him. Out, she jumped, hopped across the plush white carpet and rummaged through his dresser drawers. She pulled on one of his midnight-blue t-shirts, the color an exact match to the painted walls of his room and the bedcovers pooled on the floor at the end of his bed. At the door, she cast him a look over her shoulder as she flipped the hem of his shirt and flashed him a little of her rear. "I'll be back in five minutes."

"Make sure you are. I'm timing you." He tapped his wristwatch, his cock tenting the white cotton sheet covering his lower half, the rigid outline of his shaft visible and making her mouth water.

"I'll make it two minutes." She raced downstairs, whipped through the large living area with its black leather couches and big screen TV then skidded across the polished floorboards of the dining room toward the kitchen with its pine cupboards polished to a high sheen.

"Got you." A man stepped out of the shadows near the side door leading outside, hooked one muscled arm around her waist and clamped one hand over her mouth. Oh hell, Gair Forster was inside Brigs's home. In an inky-black wetsuit still slick with water, he leered at her, his beady black eyes pinched together. "You thought you could evade me, didn't you?"

All her survival instincts reared. She thrust her elbow into his stomach as Brigs had taught her to do during her self-defense lessons and Gair grunted, his grip loosening. She heaved around, punched her knee high into his groin and—

Another man in a wetsuit shoved her back against the wall and fisted her neck. Hugh.

She thrashed, her breath cut off but not her fighting spirit.

Gair snarled, ripped her shirt from neck to hem while Hugh continued to block her windpipe. She fought against them both, managed to yank on the burgundy curtain hanging so close. The blinds behind it rattled, and a fierce roar boomed all about.

A flash of bronze skin and Brigs moved like lightning. Gair went sailing and smashed into the dining table and wood splintered. Brigs swung his fist into Hugh's face. Blood spurted and the big brute went down and cracked his head where he landed on the hardwood floor.

"Samantha?" Brigs snagged the burgundy tablecloth and wrapped it around her shredded shirt then hauled her up against him. "Tell me you're all right, love."

"I'm all right." She gasped for breath, the air whistling painfully back down her bruised throat. "We need to find Ben and Danny."

"We're right here." Ben staggered into the room holding his bloodied head, Danny one step behind him with a gun in his hand and blood streaming from a nasty gash high across his brow.

"Did they hurt you?" She pulled Danny into her arms and hugged him hard.

"They caught us unaware while we were patrolling, knocked us both out then tied us up as well. I was guarding the front of the house and Ben the rear. We freed ourselves as quick as we could."

"I can't believe they managed to slip in." Brigs nabbed the golden tasseled ties from the curtains and tossed one set to Danny. "Let's tie these two idiots up. Ben, you call the authorities. I want them out here now and Gair and Hugh behind bars."

"You got it." Ben scooped the satellite phone from the kitchen counter and punched in the number.

Danny lugged Hugh's hands behind his back where he lay unconscious and knotted them together. Brigs bound Gair the same way then secured the bindings to his feet as well before returning to her and pulling her into his arms.

He held her fiercely tight, his voice a rough growl as he muttered, "They're down, can never hurt you again, can never take you away from me."

"You never would have let them take me away anyway." That she knew to the depths of her very soul. "You got here right on time." She cupped his face in her hands and kissed him, long and slow, just like they both needed. "I love you, Brigs. You're my bodyguard and I'm claiming you for all time."

"Just as I'm claiming you. No more hiding away for you anymore. There isn't a chance Gair's going to escape the justice coming for him, Hugh either."

She snuggled her cheek into his solid chest and clung to him and his precious words, the imprisoned men still out of it on the floor. Thankfully, with their capture, it also meant no other innocent women would ever fall prey to their devious ways.

Such relief poured through her.

It was time for her to live again, and with the very man who'd first stolen her heart so long ago. He was her bodyguard, yes, always hers.

Chapter 7

Samantha twirled on the white sand beach in front of Brigs's island mansion, her lacy summer skirt flaring out and her pink swing top fluttering. Ben, Danny, and the police had left for the main island three days ago with Gair and Hugh Forster and now both her assailants had been charged and deported to New Zealand, Ben and Danny escorting the Forsters back. Now, they'd be locked away behind bars for a very long time. Her father would ensure it. Meanwhile, she had Brigs all to herself within this tropical paradise and she didn't intend on wasting another minute of their time together.

Brigs stepped in behind her and she grinned and leaned her back against his bare chest and cuddled into his delicious hold as he wrapped his arms around her. With one hand over her belly, and the other her breasts, he whispered in her ear, "I want to get you knocked up as quick as I can."

"You do?" She turned at the serious tone in his voice, pressed a hand to his chest and counted each of the heavy and fast beats. "How come?"

"Because it's what I've always secretly wanted to do, to tie you to me in every possible way." An even more serious tone. "I want everything with you, a home and children included, which means I need you to ditch your birth control pills. Can you handle that?"

She'd always wanted children and it made no difference to her when they arrived, only that they arrived with this man as their father. "I can handle anything you decide to throw at me, your sexy body and super swimmers included."

"Good answer." His eyes glinted with desire.

"Ocean or bedroom?" She boosted up one eyebrow.

"Bedroom." He scooped her into his arms, marched up the front steps of his home, kicked the door open and strode upstairs with her. In his bedroom, he dropped her lightly onto the bed then slid in over top of her. "Before we start on the baby-making though, I have a question for you."

"And what would that be?"

"Since I never want to live without you again, I want..." He sent her one very seductive look that curled her toes. "Will you marry me, Samantha Knight?"

"Oh wow, I can't believe you're actually proposing." She looked into his beautiful brown eyes, those of the man who'd captured her heart six years ago, the only man she ever wanted to continue giving her heart to. "Yes," she whispered under her breath. "Absolutely yes. I want you in every way."

He whooped it up and she held onto her man then giggled as he dove into loving her exactly as she adored. It was time to embrace her new future, that with her bodyguard who'd always be at her side.

Thank heavens for sweet holiday flings.

Looking for more adventurous and sexy Billionaire Bodyguards?

Read on to catch a preview of the first full-length book in this series.

He will sacrifice anything to protect her.

Billionaire Bodyguards Series

Billionaire Bodyguard Attraction, Book One

Billionaire Bodyguard Boss, Book Two

Billionaire Bodyguard Fling, Book Three, Novella

JOANNE WADSWORTH

BILLIONAIRE BODYGUARD
Attraction

BOOK ONE

Chapter 1

"That is one massive super-yacht, and one I shouldn't be on." Lydia crossed her arms, eyeing the four levels of darkened glass and sleek white panels as the luxury ship sat proudly in its private berth at Auckland Marina's gated wharf. And was that a— Shoot. Yes, it was. A huge kidney shaped pool glistened from the center of the one-hundred and fifty foot yacht. All the comforts one could desire, except not her. She shouldn't even be here.

"Ben." She swung around, leveling a glare on her bodyguard.

"Don't say it." Ben scanned the marina. "You're getting on that ship and working as a caregiver. No arguments."

"Don't you 'no argument' me. Tyler Whitehall will throw me off his ship, or he would if he remembered me. What happens if he does?"

"He'll have to dive in to rescue you." He smiled then quickly straightened his mouth. "Tyler's one of the best bodyguards in the business, and I still need you somewhere safe, away from home shores. With your case unsolved, Tyler's ship is my choice."

Tyler had been assigned to guard her after she'd witnessed the hit-and-run of a wealthy businessman. Ten days later, he'd taken three bullets in the back to protect her and four-year-old

Jay. She'd never forget his blood on her hands as it had pumped from his body.

"Tyler put his life on the line for me. I won't allow that to happen again."

"Now, he wouldn't have wanted you or the boy to get hurt. That's what we do, guard."

She planted her hands on her hips. "Yes, you guard, but no, you shouldn't get shot. Not for me."

"You're an eyewitness. If we don't have you, we don't have someone to identify Johnny Taita's killer. That's when we find him. Which we will." His look was sharp, determined and inarguable. "You'll have the cover you need once on board with Tyler, as well as a break from the safe-house. Surely you like the idea of a cruise to the Fijian islands?"

She frowned. "That's a trick question. Being in The Program means remaining in seclusion. Not on board a luxury ship. Tyler's wonderful brothers and nephew will be on board. This is their family holiday."

"You'll be in more danger from Nico than he ever will be from you. Four-year-olds, as adorable as they are, are tricky little things. Nico has endless energy."

"Children aren't things."

"Same, same." He shrugged. "All that matters is you're one of the best caregivers I know. I told Nico's father, and he's all for your arrival."

"But he won't know who I am." She wanted to hit him over the head. The man was far too obstinate, and deaf. He didn't listen to a word she said. "Even Tyler won't know."

"That's the whole point of you having name suppression."

"This is impossible."

"I knew you'd come around."

What? She was not coming around, but he nudged her from behind then directed her through the arched gateway and along the slatted wooden walkway. He rolled her suitcase over the boards. Its clatter overpowered the water lapping and sloshing against the pilings.

"What I should have said was you're impossible." And a lunatic.

He chuckled. "We've lived with each other day in and day out for a year. The safe-house will ring with peace while you're gone."

"Peace my ass. I've asked Saria to ride your tail. Damn it, I can't believe I'm doing this." She yanked on his black shirtsleeve. "I mean it. I don't want to do this."

"Hey, you'll be fine. I know you're worried, but you don't need to be, and your sister's in good hands. Stop stressing, and enjoy this break. It's only on offer once."

"Tyler's on board that ship. You know the guilt I feel. I can never forget what happened to him."

"Tyler recalls nothing of his initial Program assignment with you." He pressed a hand to her back and moved her forward. "Simply assume the role of Nico's caregiver and relax. This is your chance for a little time out."

Relax? She rolled her eyes. "I can't believe I have to leave Saria behind. Do you realize twins shouldn't be separated?"

"Brigs is guarding her, and you don't have a choice."

"I could help with her correspondence study. Her nursing finals are so close."

"I'll help her." He increased his pace. "And I think by the age of twenty-one, we can safely separate you two for a month."

"We're not twenty-one, yet." Groaning, she rubbed her palms over her white cotton pants. The ship was so close. Another twenty feet and they'd reach the gangplank, and she was fresh out of arguments.

"This is where I leave." Ben halted and leaned in. "This is your chance to see Tyler as you asked for after the shooting. I know you two were…close. I couldn't grant your request then, but you're not a victim, Lydia, you're a survivor. You must live, even under confinement."

Her heartbeat raced. A year ago, she'd begged Ben to allow her to see Tyler in hospital. She'd needed to see he'd survived.

"Stop thinking and start moving, and don't forget, keep in touch on the sat phone. I expect updates as often as possible." Ben handed over her case and turned her toward the ship. "That's my girl. Now move."

"I am not your girl." Still, she flexed her fingers around the square handle of her suitcase, and taking the deepest breath, walked away from Ben for the first time in a year. She shivered. No, she could do this. A child was on board for her to look after. He was who she had to concentrate on, because her case was stagnant and the inaction wasn't doing her any good. As much as she didn't want to go, she understood Ben's arguments. She needed this break to refocus, and the Fijian Islands, wow, what a dreamy location.

She tugged at the inside of her white blouse collar then lifted her chin and eyed the ship. Up close, the white panels sparkled in the sunlight. Oh no. She slammed to a stop as Tyler stepped out from behind darkened glass sliders on the second floor. He moved across the deck to the stern, and halted ten heart-stopping feet away.

He looked strong and well, his jaw angled as firmly as always. His midnight black hair blew over his ears and brushed his shoulders. The longer length suited him over the buzz-cut he'd had last. So cute.

No. She was here for Nico, not to dance with Tyler again. That's right. Tyler must've moved on. It had been a year. She forced her thoughts under control.

* * * *

Staring out over the harbor, Tyler tucked the tails of his blue button-down shirt into his black pants. The breeze was brisk, the dawn sun warm on his skin. A perfect morning to set sail, on a family holiday he'd longed for. Liam and Nico were on board, and Dylan and Luke wouldn't be far away. These moments with his brothers and nephew mattered as much as his next breath.

Shifting onto his heels, he searched the marina for them, only his gaze landed on a young woman standing stiffly below.

Mmm, chocolate-brown hair, his favorite shade, and so long it touched her tiny waist. And those eyes, the same delicious shade, and now locked on him. Did he know her? She looked familiar, yet not. Leaning against the railing, he called, "Can I help you?"

"Um, yes. I'm after Liam Whitehall."

She was after his brother? "Who are you?"

"My name's—" Rubbing her neck, she glanced over her shoulder then back at him. "Lydia Sands. I'm Nico's new caregiver while you're on holiday. Ben Hammers arranged this job. It was short notice."

She couldn't be Nico's new caregiver. Liam would never employ anyone without running it past him first. Tyler ran all security checks, and had this past year since stepping into the security role for Whitehall Shipping. "I don't believe you."

"You should check with Liam. I promise Ben sent me." Her voice wobbled, a level of distress leaking through. "You do remember Ben, don't you?"

"Ben's impossible to forget. I worked alongside him for seven years."

"He dropped me off." She motioned toward the gated entrance, and sure enough under the intricate scrollwork of the wrought-iron arch, Ben Hammers waited. With a slow movement, Ben saluted him with just two fingers.

That salute was their team's customary silent signal for handover. But handing over whom? This woman? He didn't work for Ben, and hadn't since the shooting. Which didn't matter. The call for aid from one bodyguard to another went unquestioned, and Ben turned to leave, giving Luke a nod as he arrived.

Luke clapped Ben on the shoulder, and then continued toward him in his jeans and t-shirt. Ambling along, his youngest brother adjusted his brown leather duffel over one shoulder, as if he didn't have a care in the world, and at twenty-three, he didn't.

The woman, Lydia. He shouldn't forget her. He gripped the second-floor rail then launched over it and landed on the peer next to her.

She gasped, and her gaze jolted over him. "Tyler, what are you doing? You can't just jump off the side of a ship like that."

"Bro." Luke strode in, one brow cocked. "There's a gangplank. You know, one can walk down."

He slid between his brother and Lydia. "Yeah, I know, but Ben dropped her off. With Ben, one doesn't stroll."

"What's she here for?"

"She says she's Nico's caregiver. Have you heard about this?"

"No." Luke clicked his tongue as if telling him off. "C'mon, Liam wouldn't do that. It's too soon after Gabriella and Mum."

Their mother and Liam's wife, Gabriella, had passed only two years ago. Not one woman had been permitted on board The Idle Dream since then. This was a sacred trip between him and his brothers.

From behind, Lydia gripped his arm and a river of fire raced through his veins. Whoa. He spun and faced her. "What are you doing?" He stared at her hand.

She tucked herself in even closer, and he breathed deep.

"Tyler, I need to get inside."

Her plea spoke to his heart. "How do you know my name? You've said it twice."

A light flickered in the depths of her eyes. "Because we went out. Once."

His heart tripped a beat. Damn, he'd only ever lost a few weeks of his memory, and that was a year ago. He certainly didn't remember her. "Who the hell are you to me?"

"Someone you knew for a short time. We went on a date, and like I said, it was only once. Ben set me up for this job, of which there truly is one."

"Yeah, there wasn't a job going, Lee." He frowned. "Um, sorry, I meant Lydia." Yeah, she'd said her name was Lydia, not Lee. Only why did Lee sound more natural?

"It's okay. I had a child I cared for once who called me Lee." Her lips lifted. "Not that I'm saying you're a child."

"Ah, excuse me." Luke sighed and walked past them to the gangplank. "I feel like I'm interrupting a moment here and, bro, it's almost time for the ship to set sail."

"You're right. Let's go." Tyler held her arm and led her on board as Ben's sleek silver Jaguar revved in the parking lot. "You and Ben? You're what to each other? Are you his client?"

"No. He's a friend and got me this job. I'm not a client at all."

They walked through the opened double glass doors on the second floor and into the living room where two cozy groupings of four white leather couches faced each other. Black and white sea prints his mother had adored graced the walls painted in her favorite shade of ocean-blue.

Lydia's shoes clipped across the polished pine floors as she set her case near the stairwell. She inspected the area. "Do you mind if I ask where Liam is?"

"Below-stairs. Luke will grab him for you."

His brother groaned as he dropped his duffel on the couch. "I will?"

"Yes. Liam's downstairs checking inventory with Malcolm. Tell him we have a guest, one Lydia Sands, and bring Nico." He would see how this mysterious woman responded to his nephew, because if she wasn't a caregiver, he'd soon know.

Luke sent him a good-natured grin as he took off. "I'm onto it, only, bro, you're not to interrogate the girl while I'm gone. I see that look in your eyes."

"Just watch where you're walking." At thirty-two, he'd kept his family and countless others safe, and Ben had dropped her off. Which meant protection was required in some order, whether she was a client or not.

Leaning toward her, he met her gaze head on. "Okay, it's you and me. Now, tell me who you truly are."

* * * *

Lydia needed a sound, realistic plan because Tyler was on form as he'd always been, and she'd clearly stirred some kind of memory. From the first second, she'd sensed it, which was why she'd said they'd gone out.

"We went out for dinner. If you feel you know me, it's from then. Ben told me about your memory loss. We went out around the same time." That should put him off questioning her further.

"Are you saying"—he arched a brow—"we dated?"

"No. It was just one meal. We didn't see each other again."

"How'd we meet?" He crossed his arms.

Okay, maybe he would question her further. "Ben introduced us." And he had, but not the way she'd said. "I can't wait to meet Nico." Where was Luke?

"I'm sure you can't. How'd this dinner I can't remember go?" He came closer and touched a finger to her chin then slowly tracked it along her jaw.

"The food was nice." She swayed and almost brushed noses with him.

"Nice?"

Looking deep into his eyes, she wanted more, just as she had a year ago. "That's about it."

"That's not an answer."

Footsteps pounded up the stairwell, and she stepped back as a man's deep chuckle and a child's delighted squeal traveled to her. Luke raced around the corner carrying a squirming boy over his shoulders. "I told you I'd catch you, Nico. No Whitehall is faster than me."

"Nah-ah, Uncle Tyler's the fastest. He told me he's quicker than Superman."

"I doubt it." Luke winked at Tyler as he lowered Nico to his feet. "Superman can dodge bullets. Your Uncle Tyler hasn't nailed that essential ability yet."

Tyler laughed. "Hey, it was impossible to dodge three at once." He looked at her. "Ignore Luke. I got shot a year ago on duty, and now it makes a good joke."

"Ben told me about the shooting." Unbelievable. "Why do they joke about it?"

"It's the best way to ease the stress. I lost some memory from the time of the assignment, but the outcome was all good. I've been able to reconnect with my brothers and join Liam, Dylan and Luke at Whitehall Shipping. That wouldn't have happened otherwise."

Did he just say the outcome was all good? She tapped her ears. "I'm sorry, your memory loss must be worse than you thought if you consider being shot at as good."

"Yeah, that's not quite what I meant." With a grin, he glanced at his nephew. "Lydia, meet Nico."

She lowered to Nico's level and held out her hand. She was here for him. "Hey, Nico. I love your super-yacht."

The boy with black curls beamed. "Daddy said you were coming."

Tyler cleared his throat. "Nico, after a girl offers you her hand to shake, you never miss the opportunity to get a kiss on the cheek in too."

"Okay." Nico put his tiny hand in hers, and smacked his lips to her cheek.

She laughed. She'd missed being around children. "I'm so glad to be here."

"We're going on holiday, a big holiday." He peered over his shoulder as another man strode around the corner. This had to be Liam, so visually similar to his brothers. He had Tyler's sky-blue eyes, although Liam's dark hair was clipped short, as Tyler's used to be. Dressed in a white business shirt unbuttoned at the neck and navy dress pants, Liam crossed to her.

"Daddy, we're going on a holiday because ships are in my blood. That's what you said, but teeny-tiny ships, 'cause my blood's only little, right?"

Liam squeezed his son's shoulder. "That's kind of what I said, minus the teeny-tiny ships actually being in your blood." With a smile, he extended his hand to her. "Sorry about the late welcome. Luke told me to hurry since Tyler would have begun his interrogation. I hadn't yet had the chance to tell him you'd be traveling with us. Ben only called last night."

"It's nice to meet you, and thanks for agreeing to take me on board." She was here, and now she'd make the most of it. "Whatever you need from me, I'm here to help."

"Great. I appreciate that."

Tyler caught her arm, and drew her back to him. "Nico is almost five and he'll start school after we return. Your professional abilities will only be required until the end of this trip. Nothing beyond. Does that arrangement suit?"

"Of course. That sounds perfect." It would be impossible to have more.

With a hand at the small of her back, Tyler guided her toward the internal stairwell, and collected her bag along the way. They walked downstairs.

"Below deck are the staterooms and staff quarters, and upstairs on the third floor are Liam and Nico's suites."

"Okay." She peeked at him.

"There's a pool and spa on the top floor, and you'll be given a full tour as soon as you're settled." At the bottom of the stairs, Tyler stilled. "This dinner you say we enjoyed. I want you to know, I wish I recalled it."

"I understand about the memory loss." Okay, enough of the

non-dinner. "Oh, nice decor down here."

It truly was. Halogen lights showcased vivid blue underwater ocean scenes adorning the length of the passageway. Caramel-cream walls and plush carpet of the same color became the sandy base for all the blue.

"Thanks." Tyler moved her along. "The crew's cabins are double-bunked, but as you're the only female on board, you'll have one to yourself."

He directed her inside a small, efficient room with two bunks bolted to a blue wall. White furnishings and a built-in set of drawers completed the room.

"This is nice." She grinned, for she would love the area simply because it was all hers and totally Ben-free.

"There's a bathroom, but it connects with the cabin next door. There's a lock on each side, although the other room's empty."

Inside the compact area, she shuffled around the shower cubicle, toilet and tidy vanity, all in basic white. No frills, but she didn't need any. She met his gaze as he leaned against the doorjamb. "It's perfect."

"You seem happy." He frowned. "You appeared apprehensive to start with."

"I was nervous." She squeezed past him and returned to her room. "First day on the job and all."

She twirled in the center of her cabin. Ben was right. She needed this break.

Taken by the round portal window, she skipped toward it and peered outside. Another super-yacht of similar size to The Idle Dream came into berth, the name Star Gazer emblazoned along its side.

"It's one of ours." Tyler edged in behind her, so close.

Unable to stop, she leaned back and came up against him. Oh wow. His solid presence was like a safety blanket of warmth she'd never forget. She wanted to tip her head back, rest it on his shoulder and tell him everything, to extinguish the lie she'd told and lay out their past. Only that would never happen. Knocking that idea out of her head, she straightened. "Does Whitehall Shipping have a big fleet?"

"Twelve ships in total, but The Idle Dream was my mother's baby. It's reserved for family holidays each year. She passed away two years ago, and my father four. I don't usually speak of them, but—" He slid his fingers through her long hair. "Are you sure we didn't have more than a single date? I feel a level of comfort I can't explain."

Her thoughts swirled to the past, to those last moments she'd had with him a year ago. He'd been dressed all in black, shirt and jeans, and her heart had fluttered in her chest. They'd become so close over the ten days they'd been together, but now he was leaving. Tyler had dropped his bag in the trunk of his car and sauntered toward her.

She'd moved in his direction, and Jay had raced past and wrapped his arms around his legs. Tyler had hunkered down and hugged the boy. "I'm sorry buddy, but the rules are the rules. I can only do a ten-day rotation, but Brigs is here to look after you and Lee now."

Jay's jaw had quivered. "Could you push me on the swing one last time?"

"Sure." Tyler was such a sucker for Jay.

"But after Lee does." Jay shot a mischievous look her way.

Yeah, Jay would draw Tyler's departure out, and she understood why. Jeffrey Lawntree, his busy politician father, paid him so little attention. Tyler was a breath of fresh air for Jay, and had never left their side since his arrival. Jay loved that. She did too.

She led Jay to the old oak tree where his grandfather had knotted a tire over a high, sturdy branch.

Jay wriggled into the tire and dangled his legs over the rim, ready to go. He giggled, barely sitting still. "Go, Lee, push." Lee was his nickname for her, one she adored. Even Tyler had adopted it. Only the two of them had ever done that. So special.

Pulling both Jay and the tire, she backed up and let go when she was certain the tire would swing nice and high as Jay liked.

"It's wet, Lee," Jay yelled and laughed as he flew.

She clapped a hand against her mouth as water sloshed inside the rim. Oh no. She'd forgotten to check it first. It had rained the night before and she should have tipped it out.

"There's water in Poppa's tire and my bottom's getting wet." Jay sailed through the air, giggles exploding from him as his red shorts stained darker.

She laughed at his silly grin. "I'm so sorry."

"I can't believe you forgot." Tyler's blue eyes sparkled as he beckoned her to him. "Come and say goodbye to me."

Such husky words she couldn't ignore. "Are you finally off the clock?"

"Yes, but you're still a client."

"And a bodyguard doesn't get physical with his client?"

"It goes against the rules, Lee. It obscures our point of view."

"Rules are meant to be—" At a heavy scraping to her right, she turned. What the…

A man in green and brown camouflage gear and scraggly black hair trailing out from under his black balaclava scaled the high slatted perimeter fence. Beady black eyes sunken within yellow skin, the gaze of Johnny Taita's murderer, drilled into her. The killer from the high profile hit-and-run she'd witnessed was back. Oh hell. No way.

"Lydia." Tyler gripped her arms, dragged her back from her terrifying memories.

"I'm okay."

"Where'd you go?"

She rubbed his warm hands. Tyler was here. He was alive. He had survived.

"What took you away from me?"

"Um, bad memories. It happens sometimes. Don't you ever have those?" How could he not remember the horror of that day? It haunted her and would never leave.

"Life is too short for that sort of thing." He caressed her back. "There's something about you. You said the dinner was nice, but how did our date end?"

"Ah, it ended badly. You never called." She stepped back, only she bumped into the bunks. Then he followed her, and boxed her in. "What are you doing?"

"Go out with me again."

Go out with him for real? Could she do that?

She'd never had the chance back then, and now she was in The Program, one she wasn't leaving anytime soon. But he wasn't her bodyguard anymore. Well, not officially, and not that she would ever tell him.

"Say yes."

She looked into his eyes, and his heat radiated to every inch of her. Oh boy, she was in trouble. "I've moved on. Haven't you?"

Lies though. It was all she could offer him, no matter his answer.

"No. I have a feeling I've been waiting for you."

Her pulse tripped over itself, her heartbeat hammering out of control.

Impossible.

Love these characters and want more?

Don't miss the rest of this adventurous series.

He will sacrifice anything to protect her.

Billionaire Bodyguards Series

Billionaire Bodyguard Attraction, Book One

Billionaire Bodyguard Boss, Book Two

Billionaire Bodyguard Fling, Book Three

JOANNE WADSWORTH

BILLIONAIRE BODYGUARD *Boss*

BOOK TWO - Saria and Ben's Story.

**Also available in paperback from this author —
Scottish Historical Romance**

There can only be one…for both of them.

The Matheson Brothers Series

Highlander's Desire, Book One

Highlander's Passion, Book Two

Highlander's Seduction, Book Three

JOANNE WADSWORTH

Highlander's Desire

The Matheson Brothers Series, Book One

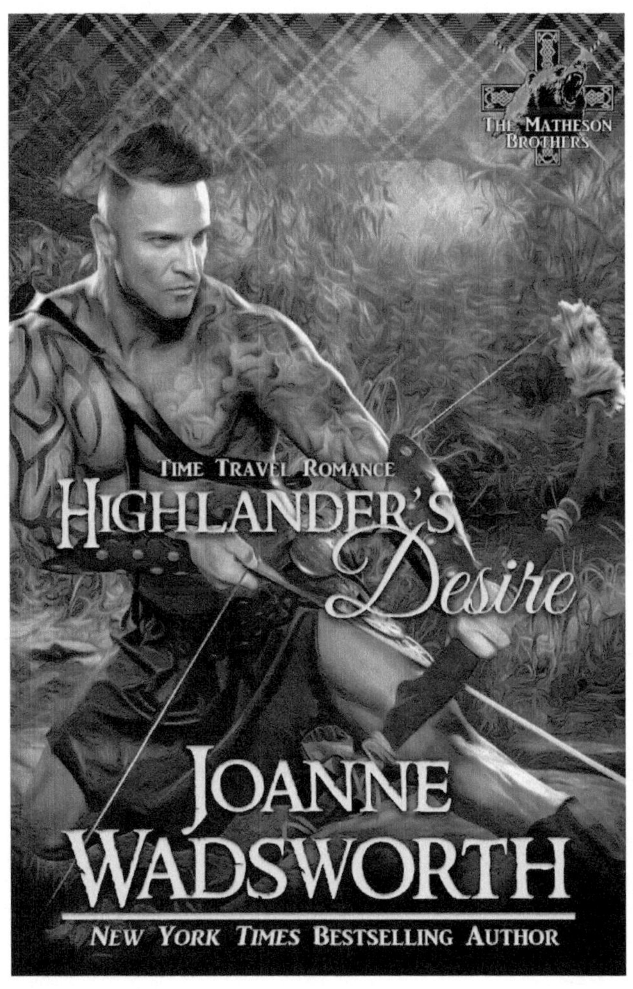

**Also available in paperback
Regency Romance**

Regency Brides Series

The Duke's Bride, Book One

The Earl's Bride, Book Two

The Wartime Bride, Book Three

The Earl's Secret Bride, Book Four

The Prince's Bride, Book Five

Her Pirate Prince, Book Six

JOANNE WADSWORTH

Regency Brides

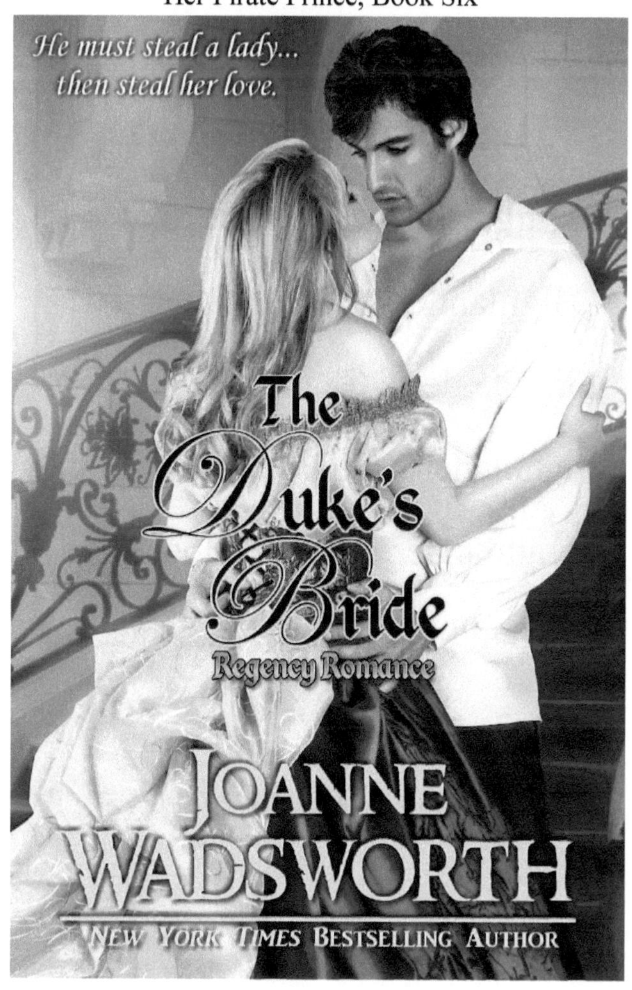

**Also available in paperback from this author —
Scottish Historical Romance**

Traveling through time…for a Highlander.

Highlander Heat Series

Highlander's Castle, Book One

Highlander's Magic, Book Two

Highlander's Charm, Book Three

Highlander's Guardian, Book Four

Highlander's Faerie, Book Five

Highlander's Champion, Book Six

JOANNE WADSWORTH

Highlander's Castle

Highlander Heat Series, Book One

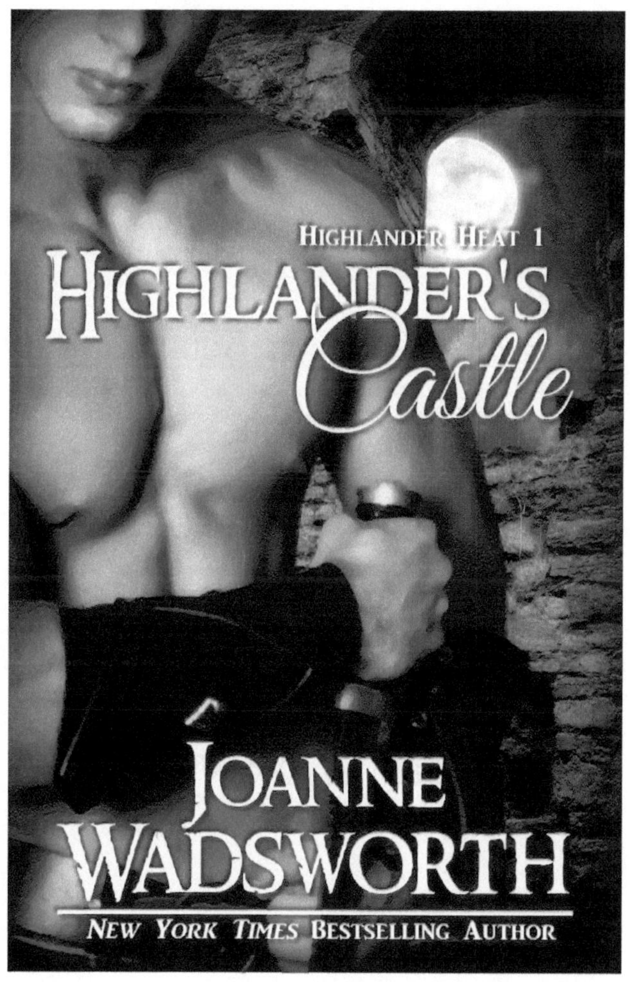

Don't miss this spell-binding Young Adult / New Adult Fantasy Romance series.

To love and protect…across worlds.

Princesses of Myth

Protector, Book One

Warrior, Book Two

Hunter, (Novella, Book 2.5)

Enchanter, Book Three

Healer, Book Four

Chaser, Book Five

JOANNE WADSWORTH

PROTECTOR

Princesses of Myth, Book One

JOANNE WADSWORTH

Joanne Wadsworth is a *New York Times* and *USA Today* Bestselling Author who adores getting lost in the world of romance, no matter what era in time that might be. Hot alpha Highlanders hound her, demanding their stories are told and she's devoted to ensuring they meet their match, whether that be with a feisty lass from the present or far in the past.

Living on a tiny island at the bottom of the world, she calls New Zealand home. Big-dreamer, hoarder of chocolate, and addicted to juicy watermelons since the age of five, she chases after her four energetic children and has her own hunky hubby on the side.

So come and join in all the fun, because this kiwi girl promises to give you her "Hot-Highlander" oath, to bring you a heart-pounding, sexy adventure from the moment you turn the first page. This is where romance meets fantasy and adventure…

To learn more about Joanne and her works, visit:
Website and Blog
http://www.joannewadsworth.com